A Dead End

Her voice was loud and ... can't figure out what hap... no clue. You've got to help...

"Slow down," Frank said gently as he joined Joe at the door. "Of course we'll help. What happened?"

"It's Dad," Kay said. Her glance darted from Joe to Frank and back to Joe again. Her voice was suddenly soft and shaky, as if she were trying to swallow her words. "He's disappeared!"

The Hardy Boys
Mystery Stories

Available from ALADDIN Paperbacks

THE **HARDY BOYS**®

#187
NO WAY OUT

FRANKLIN W. DIXON

Aladdin Paperbacks
New York London Toronto Sydney

BL: 5.5
Pts: 5.0

This book is a work of fiction. Any references to historical events,
real people, or real locales are used fictitiously. Other names, characters, places,
and incidents are the product of the author's imagination,
and any resemblance to actual events or locales or persons, living or dead,
is entirely coincidental.

First Aladdin Paperbacks edition October 2004
Copyright © 2004 by Simon & Schuster, Inc.

ALADDIN PAPERBACKS
An imprint of Simon & Schuster
Children's Publishing Division
1230 Avenue of the Americas
New York, NY 10020

The text of this book was set in New Caledonia.

Printed in the United States of America
4 6 8 10 9 7 5 3

THE HARDY BOYS MYSTERY STORIES is a trademark of Simon & Schuster, Inc.

THE HARDY BOYS and colophon are registered trademarks of Simon & Schuster, Inc.

Library of Congress Control Number 2004100584

ISBN 0-689-86738-7

Contents

NO WAY OUT

1 Bull's-Eye

The cannon explosion drowned out even the bag-pipes' drone. As the crowd jumped up and cheered, Joe Hardy felt his pulse pumping. This was going to be a great week!

He stood in the middle of the huge stadium, his arm raised out to the side. Inside his heavy leather glove, beads of sweat popped up on his fist and cascaded down his arm. He squinted against the sun, keeping his eye trained on the man standing about fifty yards away. When he heard the man's low whistle, Joe braced himself.

The man peeled the tiny leather hood off the head of the peregrine falcon perched on his arm and whistled again. Then he thrust his arm into the air.

Joe didn't move—for a few seconds, he didn't even breathe. Then the fastest bird in the world shot straight at him like a feathered bullet, its yellow talons glinting in the sun. It hit him within seconds, landing perfectly on his arm and sinking its razor beak into the chunk of steak on his glove.

Joe gulped a burst of air when he heard the man's low whistle for the third time. The falcon looked deep into Joe's blue eyes for a moment. Then its head whipped around and it rose into the air. With one powerful swoop, it folded its wings back and torpedoed to the man across the field.

Joe took a few more quick breaths, and then the crowd noise roared through his ears again. He brought his arm down and looked at the glove, now spotted with a few glistening drops of steak blood.

"Yes!" Frank Hardy exclaimed, running onto the field and clapping his brother's shoulder. "That was totally awesome!"

"Good job!" Ray and Kay Horton added in unison.

"Give them a bow or a salute or something," Kay urged. "You were a great volunteer! Most people duck when the bird flies at them."

Joe looked into the stands and waved to the spectators. "It's a pretty incredible feeling," he admitted. Then he and the others walked off the field.

It was a late spring evening on Cape Breton Island, Nova Scotia. The Hardys had known seventeen-year-old twins Ray and Kay for years, but had never been to their home, EagleSpy. The twins' father, Chezleigh Alan Horton—or Alan, as he liked to be called—was a Mazemaster, one of a few elite maze architects who had gained world recognition for their intricate and complex designs.

Alan bought the estate because the grounds included a very old maze, which had been ignored for decades. He restored and expanded the maze into one that would challenge even the toughest maze conquerors. Then he scheduled a preview week—by invitation only—of medieval games and festivities that would lead up to the public opening of the maze. When Ray invited the Hardys to the exclusive preview week, they jumped at the chance.

Frank, Joe, and the Horton twins walked toward the stands set up around the tournament stadium. As they approached, they heard the bagpipes.

"You two go up to the box," Kay said to Frank and Ray. "Joe and I will get us all some food."

Ray led Frank to the family seats, the best in the house. "The heraldry parade is supposed to start as soon as the pipers finish," he said.

"Man, what a wild group!" Frank looked around the stadium. Out on the field were sword-swallowers, jugglers, and a fire-eater up on a platform. Musicians played lutes, mandolins, and Celtic harps.

"Are you and Joe going to be in any of the maze competitions?" Ray asked Frank. "There'll be the main one, of course, plus relay races and other

3

team deals. You guys can buddy up with a couple of other entrants for the relay, if you want."

"Absolutely," Frank answered. "We're up for all of it. Joe plans to win a few prizes." The Hardys didn't look like brothers. Joe was the same age as the twins and had the same blond wavy hair and blue eyes, but Frank had short dark hair and brown eyes. Although Frank was a year older and a couple of inches taller, Joe was more athletic.

Joe and Kay returned to the box with snacks for all. "So, are we having fun yet?" Kay yelled over the noise. A late-afternoon breeze filtered through her sun-streaked hair.

"Definitely," Frank said with a wide grin as Joe and Kay sat down in their bleacher seats. He started to say something, but gave up trying. The bagpipers were winding back up to an even higher pitch, and all talk was useless. Even the television broadcasters had stopped filing their reports in front of bright lights and grinding videocams down on the field.

Men and women dressed like medieval knights, ladies, swordsmen, and peasants were sprinkled throughout the stands and on the stadium field below. Brigands, reivers, and archers swaggered through the gathering. Many of the spectators wore masks, hoods, or armor helmets. The falconer stood off by himself, his hooded raptor perched like a statue on his fist. Joe felt a rush as he remembered the bird landing on his wrist.

"Are we on TV?" Frank asked the twins. He pointed to a couple of men with video cameras. "Or is Alan recording all of this?"

"You guessed it," Ray said. "Dad hired them."

"That studio's pretty famous around here," Kay said. "They do documentaries for clients all over the world. Dad's thinking he might put together a series on mazes and market it to some cable station."

"Excellent," Joe said. From his seat he could see the medieval bazaar in the large meadow between the stadium and the maze. Hundreds of vendors had set up booths and tables to sell authentic, and reproductions of, medieval wares.

The opening parade began with a blast of long herald trumpets. Alan and his wife, Penny, leading a double column of special guests and dignitaries, rode through the stadium on horses draped with colorful cloths and sporting long, flowing ribbons braided through their manes and tails.

After the parade, the Hardys and the twins watched a jousting demonstration. But they left early to help Alan set up for the ribbon-cutting.

"Good job with the falcon, Joe," Penny said when they arrived.

"I'll say," Alan agreed. He clapped Joe's shoulder in a firm grip. "Now give me a hand with this platform."

"The opening event in the maze is a relay," Kay explained to the Hardys. "And the teams will all be from the international press corps that Dad invited. It'll be fun."

"And great publicity," Penny added with a wink.

By the time the rest of the spectators arrived at the maze, twilight had crept over the horizon, swallowing up the last rays of the sun. Everyone gathered in front of the nine-foot outer hedge wall. The opening was draped in a purple cloth. The curtain was bordered by swaying poles of heraldic banners and by authentic twenty-foot-high medieval torches that shot flames toward a sky flushed with gray and orange.

Alan stood on a small platform near the maze entrance so everyone could see him while he made his opening remarks.

"My dear friends and colleagues," he began, "as you all know, mazes and labyrinths have been unearthed in the ruins of nearly all cultures across the globe. They date back to 1800 B.C. This maze is not that old, but I feel as though I've been working on it nearly that long!"

The crowd joined in Alan's laughter.

"As most of you know, I've worked on this maze design for nearly four years. The basics of a unique puzzle were already here, but I've added a few touches of my own."

"No surprises there, eh, mate?" a voice called from the crowd, which responded with cheers and hoots of approval. Frank looked back through the gathering. The caller was a man Ray had pointed out earlier, a maze specialist from Australia.

"Some of you know me pretty well," Alan said, nodding and grinning at the crowd. "That's why you're here. Except for you, ladies and gentlemen of the press, this group represents the fiercest maze competitors in the world, and even a few true Mazemasters. I'm proud and honored that you have accepted my invitation to try your hand at this creation. I consider it my masterpiece."

Another cheer exploded from the crowd.

"As I told you in the invitation, the main competition will be a form of a scavenger hunt. You'll need just three tools to win it: your experience with labyrinths, your proven acute powers of observation, and a Global Positioning System receiver. Most of you probably brought your own GPS. I have a few to lend, if necessary. And for those of you who are interested, embedded journalists will race with you." He gestured toward the men with cameras.

The Hardys nodded at each other. They had the latest version of GPS units, and had used them a couple of times to help solve crimes.

"The invitation did not mention the prizes that will be awarded to those who solve the maze puzzle," Alan continued.

The crowd hushed. "Wait till you hear this," Kay

whispered to the Hardys with a wide grin. "It's spectacular."

"The maze champion in the scavenger hunt competition will be awarded this." Alan reached into a large velvet bag hanging from his shoulder and pulled out a shiny object. He held it up, and a golden glow shot off rays in the light of the blazing torches. "It's one of the treasures from my personal collection," he announced. "An authentic gilded gauntlet from medieval Scottish heraldry. My ancestor won this gauntlet from an archrival in a jousting match like the ones we'll have here tomorrow. And you will have the opportunity to win the gauntlet from me by solving my maze and its puzzle."

The crowd erupted into a third cheer. "What's that noise?" Joe said to his brother.

"You're kidding, right?" Frank called back over the rollicking shouts of the spectators.

"No . . . not the crowd noise," Joe said. "Listen!"

The cheers died down, and Frank heard an odd whistling sound that accompanied Alan as he continued to explain the rules of the competition.

"Is it the bagpipers winding up for the ribbon-cutting?" Frank murmured.

"I don't think so," Joe answered. "It sounds more like something flying, like something in the air, like—"

Golden-red sparks rained down on the crowd.

People began slapping at their clothes and hair and at the people standing near them, snuffing out tiny embers. The whistling grew louder as a flaming arrow shot over the crowd in a perfect arc and landed in the maze wall.

2 A Knight in the Woods

When the blazing arrow landed in the hedge wall, it flickered for a moment, and then fanned into flames.

The crowd quickly divided into three groups. Some panicked and ran away. The reporters took notes, spoke into backpack recorders and cameras, and filmed the growing fire. Others raced to help squelch the flames.

"Come on," Joe said to Frank. "I think the arrow came from the bleachers. The archer could have hustled up to one of the top rows so he could get a clear view."

The Hardys hurried toward the stadium, reversing the direction the arrow had taken. A lot of people were running in all directions, so they had to fight to follow their route.

"Let's split up," Frank suggested. "You go around that way, and I'll take the east side. Be sure to scan under the bleachers. Look for signs of a small fire. The archer had to light the arrow somewhere."

They took separate paths around the field.

Frank divided his search between weaving in and out under the bleacher stands and gazing over the field and the meadows beyond. He saw nothing suspicious. Finally, he met up with Joe at the opposite end of the field.

"Nothing," Joe declared.

"Me neither," Frank said. He peered out around the perimeter of the meadow to the edge of the forest. "He could be anywhere by now."

"I know—and he still could be here, too," Joe pointed out. "Just milling around with everyone else, or even helping to put out the fire. We don't have a clue."

"Let's go back," Frank conceded. "They might need our help at the maze."

As they hurried back across the field, Joe saw a rush of silver in his peripheral vision. He turned quickly and squinted into the dim light around a dense woods in the distance. "Do you see something over there?" he asked his brother. "There . . . toward the trees."

Frank looked in the direction Joe pointed. "No, I don't see anything. What is it?"

"I'm not sure," Joe said. "Looked like somebody

11

disappearing into the woods—somebody in silver."

"Like someone dressed in chain mail armor?" Frank said, taking off with a burst of energy. Joe was close behind.

The Hardys sprinted toward the woods. When they got to the edge, Frank heard crunching twigs, and a swishing sound like something brushing against the leaves. They followed as far as they could until the forest was too dense and dark to navigate.

Frank grabbed Joe's arm and shook his head. He knew that without light they'd be foolish to go any farther. They could walk into a dangerous trap.

"Let's go back," Joe whispered, as if he'd read Frank's mind. He turned around and began retracing his steps out of the woods. With each step, he scanned the ground and the surrounding shrubs and weeds. They saw some trash left by the costumed spectators, but nothing that looked like it could be a clue to their quarry's whereabouts or identity.

As they hurried back to the maze, Frank stopped suddenly. "Wait a minute," he said. "I've got an idea." He led Joe over to a platform that had been rolled to the edge of the field.

"The fire-eater!" Joe said. "Of course. Whoever shot that arrow could have used his platform."

"And used the fire-eater's equipment to flame the arrow."

The platform was empty, and there was no sign of the trunk that contained the flammable liquids, ignition devices, and wands that the fire-eater slid down his throat.

When the Hardys arrived at the edge of the maze wall, the fire was nearly extinguished. A small truck from the local village had arrived and pumped steady pulses of water onto the hedge. The crowd had thinned, but those who remained crowded around Alan and his family, consoling them and offering their help and support.

"What happened to you guys?" Ray asked as the Hardys joined them. "I saw you running toward the woods."

"We tried to run down the archer," Joe explained. He and Frank told Ray where they'd been and what they'd seen.

"Where's the fire-eater?" Frank asked. "Is he still around?"

"I saw him just a few minutes ago," Kay said, scanning the small crowd. "There he is." She pointed to a tall man with a long dark ponytail, still dressed in his orange and yellow costume, helping the firefighters drag the hose a few feet. The Hardys and the twins pitched in to help.

Finally the fire was out, and all the smoking embers were stamped into dust. Frank wandered over to talk to the fire-eater, and Joe and the Hortons walked to the maze to look over the damage.

"What a mess," Alan said, riffling through the seared hedge. The outer wall of the maze was pierced with a huge burned-out hole, nearly three yards square. Joe and Ray helped him sift through some of the piles of ashes and charred branches. At last Alan stood up, shaking his head. He handed the bag containing the gilded gauntlet to Penny Horton and asked her to take it back to the house. Then he clenched his teeth and stormed to the platform where he'd given his earlier speech.

"Well, you all can see what's happened here," he said. "Someone has tried to destroy the maze and put a stop to all your fun. Well, we're not going to allow that to happen!" The crowd that remained was smaller than the original one, but made nearly as much noise as they cheered him on.

"We'll have to postpone the opening of the maze for a day or two until we can restore the wall with new hedges. But that doesn't mean that all the festivities must be put on hold. Tomorrow morning the tournament matches, medieval games, and bazaar will go on as planned. Pass the word to those who have already left, get some sleep, and be back here tomorrow, ready to play!"

As the remaining onlookers filed off, Alan went over to talk to a village policeman, Officer Chester. Joe followed and listened to their conversation.

After Alan had given the officer all the information he had about the flaming arrow, Joe spoke up.

"I think I saw someone going into the woods. He was big and was dressed in something flashy and silver, but I didn't get much of a look at his face. Come to think of it, I'm not even sure it was a man."

"Several people saw someone fitting that description disappear into the forest," the officer informed him, nodding toward a couple helping Alan with the cleanup. "But, like you, no one saw the face or any other distinguishing features. You didn't see the person's hair, for instance?"

"No, I didn't," Joe answered.

"Well, then," Officer Chester said, flipping his notebook closed. "That doesn't give us much, now does it?"

Joe and Alan went back to help Ray, Kay, and the others clean out some of the burned remains. Frank joined them, and Kay questioned him as soon as he walked up. "I saw you talking to the fire-eater," she said. "What was that all about?"

"Just a hunch," Frank said. "He said he's from Newfoundland. Has anyone found anything here?"

"No," Alan answered. "It's getting dark and I'm feeling a little jumpy. I think I'll check the interior of the maze."

"I'll go with you, Dad," Ray said.

"Do you need some help?" Joe asked.

"That depends," Ray asked. "Are you still planning to compete in the maze scavenger hunt?"

"Sure," Joe answered. "I've got my GPS primed and ready to go."

"That's what I figured," Ray said, with a half smile. "So you're not getting anywhere near the inside now. You'll see it for the first time when all the other contestants do."

"I get it," Joe said. "Wasn't thinking, I guess."

While the others watched, Alan unlocked a small steel shed hidden in the hedges on the outside of the maze and stepped inside. He opened the combination lock of a small safe encased in cement and punched a few numbers onto a keypad inside the safe. An eerie glow appeared above the maze.

"Cool, isn't it?" Kay commented as she followed Joe's gaze to the glow over the hedges. "We've got lights embedded in the hedges every few yards. The maze isn't fully lit, but you can still walk it at night and see where you're going."

Alan fiddled with the keypad another few seconds.

"He's turning off the alarm system?" Frank guessed.

"Right," Kay answered. "He's not only got alarms at the gate, he's got motion sensors scattered throughout the whole maze."

Alan closed the shed door and he and Ray disappeared inside the hedge wall. Frank and Joe pulled on heavy cotton gloves that Kay handed them, and began running their hands slowly through the

16

ashes. Kay followed their lead. Occasionally, someone would feel something weird and pull it out, but it was just a rock or a twig.

Then Frank's fingers closed around something very straight and very smooth. "I've got something," he announced. He pulled it out of the pile in a cloud of powdery gray ashes, and wiped it off on his jeans.

"That's the arrow," Kay said. "It has to be."

"Well, it's definitely an arrow shaft," Joe said.

"It's iron or steel—iron, probably, because it looks really old," Frank guessed. He polished it with a rag that Kay had handed to him. "Look, there's something marked on here," he said, pointing to the broken end. "A design of some kind. It's like a family crest or a tribal insignia. But it's so worn, it's hard to make out."

"There might be some words," Kay said, looking closely. "Or maybe it's just a picture."

"Check that out," Joe said, pointing to a series of lines. "What's that?"

Frank spit on the rag and rubbed the arrow shaft with the wet cloth. "It looks like a *B*," he said.

"It's in Old English script," Joe said, "like the kind of printing they did in medieval times."

"You're not going to believe this!" Ray yelled, bursting through the burned-out hole of the hedge. "Inside, in the center of the maze . . . ," he said, panting between words, "it's trashed!"

17

3 The Hidden Passage

"How do you mean 'trashed,' exactly?" Frank asked.

"I mean someone's been inside the maze," Ray said. "And destroyed the center. The niches, the benches, the banner poles, the mailbox—everything's been knocked over, dug up, or smashed."

But how could someone get in without our knowing it?" Kay asked. "We installed that major security system." She looked toward the shed where Alan had turned off the security alarm before he and Ray had gone into the maze.

"Well, it didn't do me any good, did it!" Alan said. Each word exploded out of his mouth like a miniature firework.

"This is going to put off the opening even longer," Kay said. "What are we going to do?"

"We're going to clean it up," Alan said, gazing through the opening at the next wall of the maze. "We'll need two days, at least. Tomorrow at the games I can make an announcement about the maze opening. Not a word to anyone about the mess inside the maze," he added, glaring at his children. "Understand? This doesn't go beyond our family— and that includes you," he said to the Hardys.

"What about the police?" Frank asked.

"I'll report it eventually," Alan said. "I need time to think first. And I don't want the press to get a hold of this yet."

"Do you have any idea who might have done it?" Joe asked Alan and Ray. "Did you see anything in there that could be a clue?"

"Nothing," Ray said. "We'll look again tomorrow morning."

"I found something out here in the ashes," Frank told Alan and Ray, pointing out the area where he'd found the faint design. He handed Alan the arrow shaft.

Alan rubbed his thumb against the worn lines and held up the shaft in the light from the still-burning torches. "This looks like a *B*," he muttered. "Thanks—I'll hold on to it." Then he stuffed the arrow into his belt and stormed into the shed to turn on the alarm system. "Whatever it takes, this maze is going to open!" he declared, locking the shed door.

They hurried back to the house, where Penny

had coffee and cherry cobbler waiting on the wood-and-steel island in the huge kitchen.

"I need to talk to you," Alan said to Penny. "We'll be in the library," he said to the others, guiding Penny out of the kitchen.

The Hardys pulled some stools up to the island and pumped the twins for information.

"Your dad didn't seem to be surprised to see the *B* on the arrow shaft," Frank said. "Do you think he has a suspect in mind?"

"Vincenzo Blackstone," the twins said in unison.

"He thinks he's so much better than Dad," Kay said. "But he's not even close. Dad *always* beats him out—always has!"

"I take it he's also a Mazemaster?" Joe guessed.

"He'd like to think so," Ray said. "But it's not true. He's not half the designer Dad is—never will be."

"He's okay," Kay said. "Dad has even thought that some of his mazes are pretty cool. But he's such a—"

"Creep." Ray finished his sister's thought, then went back to eating his cobbler.

"Blackstone has a major temper," Kay explained. "I mean, it's really violent. We've only seen him a few times—at special maze exhibitions, and a few competitions. Once, we were at a gig in Scotland and Blackstone jumped one of the maze architects. They had this huge fight, and the other guy ended up in the hospital with a broken arm. Vincenzo paid a huge fine, but he wasn't thrown out of the competition."

"Who won?"

"Dad did, of course," Kay said with a big grin.

"That's not the only time Vincenzo's been in trouble, though," Ray pointed out. "It's common knowledge that he once hired a bunch of guys to destroy a rival's maze."

"The other guy had won an Asian competition," Kay added.

"Yeah, and Blackstone thought that *he* deserved to win instead," Ray continued. "So he had the winner's maze totally destroyed."

"What happened?" Frank asked. "Was he arrested?"

"There wasn't enough evidence to even hold him," Ray explained.

"Do you think he's here now?" Joe asked. "Here on Cape Breton Island? Would he come for the games and the opening of your dad's maze?"

"Well, he sure wasn't invited," Kay said. "But that wouldn't keep him from showing up."

"Looks like we need to find out if he's around," Frank said, exchanging looks with Joe.

"You're thinking the *B* on the arrow shaft might stand for *Blackstone*?" Joe asked.

"Makes sense to me," Ray said, gulping down his coffee.

"What does this guy look like?" Frank asked.

"He's kind of average," Kay answered. "Medium height, medium weight. Dark hair and eyes."

A picture of the burly figure running into the woods skittered through Joe's mind. "Does he ever wear a costume at these tournaments—like armor or chain mail? Anything like that?"

"No way!" Ray said. "He never participates in jousting matches or anything like that. He's only interested in mazes. He considers himself a real artist."

"*I* consider him a snake," Kay muttered, "and a common criminal. And I'm not the only one with that opinion."

"The gauntlet that your dad has put up for the maze prize is so cool," Joe said, changing the subject. He could see that Kay was getting really heated up.

"Definitely," Ray agreed. "You can have a closer look tomorrow and even see how it fits."

"It might give you a little extra incentive to win," Kay added with a teasing smile.

"I'm surprised he's giving away a family heirloom," Frank said. "It's something that's been passed down in your family for centuries. And he'd just give it away like that."

"He's got tons of stuff like that," Kay said. "We've got a barrel of gauntlets from our ancestors. Our family's been collecting this stuff for centuries."

"Yes, and we have crates and rooms full of other stuff," Ray said. "Dad's second obsession, after mazes, is medieval and renaissance heraldry. He loves all the legends and myths about knights and swash-bucklers. And he's added a lot of artifacts to the family heirlooms—suits of armor, jousting equipment, banners, and more."

"Eventually he wants to build a museum to house all his stuff," Kay pointed out. "Right now it's in warehouses all over the island."

"And in Halifax," Ray added.

"And Scotland," Kay said. "It's probably the world's largest private collection of medieval artifacts."

"Outside of collections owned by various royal families, of course," Kay pointed out.

It had been a late night, and everyone agreed that a hot shower and a warm bed was just what they wanted. With a pledge to the twins to find the person who had declared war on their father and his maze, the Hardys went upstairs to their guest suite.

"Vincenzo Blackstone is a perfect suspect," Joe concluded. He and Frank had cleaned up, and then flopped into their beds in the large bedroom. "He's got a track record of an attack on another maze—"

"*Alleged* attack," Frank interrupted. "Ray and Kay said it was 'common knowledge' that he hired those thugs to do it. But there was no real evidence, no indictment, no trial."

"Okay, okay," Joe conceded. "You're right. But it sounds as if the twins are not the only ones who think he was guilty. And they have seen his violent temper firsthand. Plus, he's supposed to be jealous of other Mazemasters."

"You heard his description, though," Frank said. "He didn't sound like the guy you saw running away after the flaming arrow was shot."

"True, but I didn't get a very clear view of him. And he could have been wearing a bulky costume. Lots of the spectators are completely disguised. Besides, if Blackstone was behind this, he could have hired someone else to shoot the arrow. He seems to have a history of hiring other people to do his dirty work—"

"Allegedly," Frank interrupted again.

"All right, all right," Joe said. "I still say we check him out first thing tomorrow. What did the fire-eater say? Any chance the archer could have used his stuff to light the arrow?"

"He didn't think so," Frank said. "He told me he's really careful about his equipment because it could be dangerous in the wrong hands. It's usually locked up tight, and he's aware of its whereabouts all the time. When he finishes his act, his stuff gets locked up in his truck right away. That's what he did tonight. He checked it right after the arrow was shot, just in case. But everything was secure."

"Okay, then," Joe said. "It's on to Mr. Blackstone first thing tomorrow. Agreed?"

"Agreed," Frank said.

"First thing," Joe repeated in a faint mumble.

The next thing Frank heard coming from his brother's bed was a familiar snore.

Frank finally fell asleep, but not for long. He kept waking up, and wasn't sure why. As he lay in the plush bed, he heard a low racket of weird noises. The Hortons had done a great job of restoring the ancient wood-and-stone mansion. But they hadn't gotten rid of its groans and creaks and the *tap-tap-tap* sounds that interrupted the late night quiet.

As he continued trying to go back to sleep, Frank made a game of listening for a noise and then identifying its source. *That's the wind moving through the wooden beams,* he guessed, after an eerie moaning noise. He heard a strange crackling, and then a sort of grinding crunch. He pictured the big stones that supported the lower half of the house. *They're scraping against one another as the house settles,* he told himself.

It was silent for a few minutes, and Frank felt himself sliding back into sleep. But then a steady *creak . . . creak . . .* behind his headboard yanked him back awake. He sat up and stared at the wall over his shoulder, following the noise that moved back and forth behind the wall.

"Joe!" Frank whispered, looking over toward his brother's bed. "Joe, are you awake?"

"Mglblffft." Joe's snore answered the question.

"Okay, guess the fun's all mine this time," Frank muttered. He slid out from under the covers and pulled on a pair of jeans over his sleep shorts. He stuffed his penlight into his pocket and crossed the room in his bare feet. A creepy tremor rippled through him. The room was unfamiliar, and filled with a dense darkness.

He reached the door and stretched out his hand for the slick brass doorknob. Clenching it firmly, he inched it around until he heard a tiny click.

The door opened to the faint yellow of the hall night-light. As air was pushed outward, dust particles swirled through the dusky amber glow. He peered into the hallway and strained to hear every sound. He looked back into the bedroom for a few seconds to get his bearings, checked where his headboard was, and then visualized how that matched up with the other rooms on the floor as he looked into the hallway.

The main hall was twenty feet wide and stretched at least sixty or seventy feet to a carved mahogany staircase winding down to the first floor. Several smaller corridors stemmed from the main hallway and seemed to lead to other wings of rooms.

"The room on the other side of my headboard has to be down that hall," Frank told himself as he eyed the entrance to a nearby smaller corridor.

He stepped onto the carpet leading away from his room and ducked around the corner into the smaller passageway. The hall had no light of its own, and he had to make his way in the glow from the chandelier behind him.

There was only one doorway on the left, and he knew immediately that it led to whatever was on the other side of his bed. Frank turned the knob and opened the door to a medium-size room. It was very dark but not totally black, thanks to a faint light on the opposite wall. Shadowy legs paced slowly back and forth in the light.

Frank ducked back behind the partially open door for a few seconds, plotting his attack. He peeked back into the room. The light still shone from the opposite wall, but the shadow was no longer moving in it. Frank strained his hearing, but there was no sound, so he stepped silently inside the room.

Bare feet, he told himself. *Good move*.

Following the wall with one hand, he crept around the room. When he got to the opposite side, he discovered that the light had been coming from behind a closet door that was slightly ajar. He still heard nothing but his own heavy heartbeat and the groans and rattles of the house.

He stopped for barely a second to take a quiet breath and try to slow down his pulse. Then he peeked into the closet.

A row of costumes hung from a high rod, and he was startled to see that the bulb hanging from the closet ceiling was not on. The light was coming from the back of the closet, so the heavy clothes were backlit.

He paused again, but still heard nothing except quick bursts of air from his own nostrils. He reached up and moved first one garment, then another, to reveal an open door hidden in the back wall of the closet. The light he'd seen came from beyond that door and up a short, narrow flight of ten steps. For a moment he thought he saw the shadows of someone's legs pacing at the top of the stairs, but they disappeared.

Frank cautiously placed the bare toes of his left foot on the first step and leaned forward. Relieved to hear no creaking response from the wooden plank, he pulled his full weight forward and started up the secret passageway.

It was so narrow, his shoulders brushed against both side walls as he moved slowly upward, one cautious step at a time. He had to duck his head and shoulders to keep from grazing the ceiling above. When he stepped onto the third tread, he felt a sharp twinge in his heel. He reached down and felt the edge of the step. It was splintered away into sharp shards of wood. He rubbed his heel and then started up again.

He held his breath when he reached the halfway point. He knew that when he rose onto the sixth step he would be able to get his first glimpse of whatever was waiting at the top.

He crouched down a little farther and placed his foot on the sixth step. He felt another sharp twinge. But this one was in his shoulder—and it came from the fingers that had clamped on to it.

4 The Gauntlet Is Thrown

His heart booming through his chest, Frank spun around, trying to knock the hand off his shoulder.

"Alan!" he said, recognizing his host's face in the dim light. "What are you . . . where did . . . how?" Frank stopped to inhale a gulp of air. "I didn't know you were still up," he finally said.

"I couldn't sleep," Alan answered. "I heard some strange noises and thought I'd take a look. You startled me."

"Yeah . . . well . . . same here."

Alan's hand remained on Frank's shoulder, and he felt a gentle pressure moving him back down the steps. It was clear that Alan wanted him away from the staircase.

"Do you have any other guests staying in the

house?" Frank asked his host as he reluctantly followed him down the staircase.

"No, why?" Alan didn't hesitate before answering, but he didn't seem surprised by the question either. They walked through the closet and back into the main room.

"I thought I saw the shadow of someone pacing back there," Frank answered, nodding toward the secret passageway. He decided not to tell Alan about the sounds he'd heard from his bed—the sounds that had started him on the search.

"It was probably me," Alan said, still guiding Frank firmly down the small corridor. "I've been up for hours. All this mess with the maze . . . I've got to figure out who's doing this."

They finally reached the main hall. "You probably just saw shadows—maybe tree branches through a window or something," Alan pointed out.

"Mmmm," Frank said, looking around.

"Hey," Alan said, his expression brightening. "Maybe it was just a ghost. All the old houses on Cape Breton have them. Why should this one be any different, eh?"

They had arrived at the door to the Hardys' guest suite. "You'd better get some sleep, now," Alan said. "You want to be rested and fit for the tournament tomorrow morning, don't you?"

"Sure," Frank said. "You're right." He could tell there was something going on that Alan wasn't telling him, and that he was definitely in the way. But he could also tell he wasn't going to get any more information about the secret staircase from Alan at that moment. So he changed the subject.

"By the way," he said as Alan started to move away from the door. "The twins told us you're filming all the activities this week."

"I am," Alan said, turning back. "And we've got an ace studio doing the work. I can't wait to see how they cut it."

"I'd like to see the rough print of tonight's filming as soon as possible," Frank said. "Joe and some others saw a man running into the woods right after the flaming arrow was shot. We're hoping the filmmakers caught it and we can get an ID."

"I'll give you the names and numbers in the morning," Alan said. "But I've already talked to them. They got no shots of the archer with the flaming arrow."

"That's okay," Frank said. "There might be something else that will help." He said good night and went back into his room.

He heard Alan walk down the hall. Opening the door just a couple of inches, Frank saw Alan turn the corner to the small corridor leading to the hidden door in the closet. *I'm going back up there,* Frank promised himself, *but not tonight.*

When he plunked onto the bed this time, he fell asleep.

✧ ✧ ✧ ✧

"Come on!" Joe's voice drilled into Frank's ears. "It's eight o'clock. The games start in two hours. We've got to get organized."

Frank felt his dream slipping away as the Saturday morning sun shone on his eyelids. "Hey," he grunted, sitting up. "I was having the weirdest dream. I couldn't sleep, so I got up and wandered around the second floor and saw this guy . . . no, Alan . . . no, this guy *and* Alan . . . that was after the hidden door in the back of the closet that led to a little stairway . . . and Alan said the guy was a ghost, but I didn't believe him, and—"

"Whoa. Slow down," Joe called from the bathroom. "Alan was a ghost on a hidden stairway? That's some dream."

"No, Alan said the *other* guy was a ghost. Wait a minute. It wasn't a dream." Frank stood and scratched his shoulder. "It happened."

While they cleaned up and got dressed, Frank told his brother about his midnight exploration.

"Are you really sure you saw these shadows?" Joe asked him.

"Well, yeah . . . I think so." Frank replayed the whole scene in his mind.

"And it wasn't Alan?" Joe said.

"How could it be? He caught me from behind, so he wasn't up there."

"Unless there's another way to get in and out of that room," Joe said.

33

"Right," Frank agreed. "That's definitely possible. An old house like this probably has lots of hidden passageways and secret rooms. I'd like to get up there and scope it out. Maybe later—when we're sure the Hortons are all out of the house. In the meantime, we need to find out who's trying to destroy Alan's maze."

"I wish I'd gotten a better look at that guy who ran into the woods," Joe said as he combed his hair. "I'd like to compare stories with other witnesses. When I talked to Officer Chester, he pointed out a couple of people who were helping Alan with the cleanup last night. They live in town—Harold and JoAnne Donaldson. They also reported a man running away, but they left before I could talk to them. The twins can probably help me track them down."

"Good. And don't forget, Alan has those documentary filmmakers on the job. He's giving me their names this morning. Maybe the running guy was caught on camera last night."

"Excellent," Joe said.

"I also want to find out more about Vincenzo Blackstone. A lot of the people here probably know who he is, and someone might know whether he's around the island. Ray and Kay can tell me who'd be the most likely person to know where he is."

"We can start that search right now," Joe said, "and pull up some preliminary stuff from my laptop."

"Great, let's get going," Frank urged. "Maybe we

can get some work done before the jousting matches start later this morning."

"I don't want to miss those," Joe said. "The Hortons have picked out horses for us and set up some training and practice times."

Frank led the way. Joe grabbed his notebook computer and followed quickly.

Over a quick breakfast with the twins, Joe searched the Internet for Blackstone. "He's got a pretty flashy Web site," Joe reported to the others.

"I'm not surprised," Kay said. "He's *all* about flash."

"And not much to back it up," Ray added.

"He's got a whole calendar of appearance dates and a maze-architect schedule," Joe continued. "Nothing here about coming to Cape Breton, though, or any mention of your dad's festival."

"Also no surprise," Kay muttered.

While Joe clicked away in the background, the twins gave Frank names and descriptions of people he could ask about Blackstone's whereabouts.

Joe finally closed his computer. "I managed to get his e-mail addresses and his telephone numbers," he said with a grin, "and even his cell phone number. We can contact him directly, if we want."

"You're a genius hacker," Frank said, copying the numbers into his PDA. "First, let's see if we can track him down without him knowing about it," Frank said.

"I haven't told you the best part," Joe said. "Turns out he has a U.S. driver's license, which I copied onto this CD. Point me to a printer, and I can get us some mug shots to work with."

"There's one in my room," Ray said. "Help yourself."

Joe took the disc from his computer and printed out a dozen copies of Vincenzo Blackstone's face on Ray's printer.

"Yuck, that's definitely him," Kay said when Joe returned with the mug shots.

"This is great," Frank said. "I'm going to work the crowd with these—flash them around and see whether anyone's spotted him."

"I'll go with you," Ray said. "Oh, Dad asked me to give you this card. It's for the film studio. Skip Jennin is the assistant director, and Dad told him to give you whatever you want."

"Perfect," Frank said, pocketing the card. "Okay, I'm out of here. See you at eleven at the stables," Frank told Joe. "Jousting practice . . . don't forget!"

"You'll love the horses we picked out for you," Ray said. "They're really good with strangers and with the crowds on the field. But I know you both have ridden a lot, so they're pretty lively, too."

"I'm so happy you guys are here," Kay said as she watched Frank leave. "Dad's been planning this event for years. He's put all his energy and creativity—"

"And money—" Ray interjected.

"And *heart*," Kay continued, "into restoring the maze and sharing it with people. It's just *got* to be a success. Please don't let some jealous jerk ruin it!"

"We're on it," Joe assured her. "Don't worry."

Joe grabbed his computer and headed back up to the guest suite to drop it off. He pulled a light-weight blue sweater over his T-shirt and left the room. As he walked back toward the large, sweeping staircase, he peered down the small corridor that Frank had followed in the middle of the night.

Joe looked around. There was no one else on the second floor he could see or hear, so he headed straight for the door that Frank had told him about. It was unlocked, so he stepped into the room. He waited for a minute, but he heard nothing.

Remembering the description that Frank had given, Joe headed straight across the room to the closet with the medieval costumes. He pulled the hanging clothes aside to reveal the hidden door in the back wall of the closet. It was wide open, and the small stairway was awash with light from the room above. Joe heard someone pacing back and forth just beyond the top of the stairs. The sound suddenly stopped, and a familiar voice called out.

"Is someone down there?" Joe heard Alan say. "Who's there—Kay? Ray?"

"It's Joe. May I come up?"

Alan walked to the top step and stared down at

Joe. "Might as well," he said. "I give up. I should have known that I couldn't keep the famous Hardys from scoping out my hiding place. You guys are even better detectives than Ray told me you were."

At the top of the staircase, Joe stepped into a small room. There were no windows and no other doors that Joe could see. A small desk and chair anchored one corner, and a comfy-looking chair and a bookcase full of old books filled the opposite corner. A long artist's table ran the length of one wall, lit by a lamp with a small fan hanging from the ceiling. A few large pieces of paper lay on top of the far end of the table. From where Joe stood, they looked like engineering schematics or diagrams.

"This is my little retreat," Alan said. "A place to get away and do some thinking or reading."

"It's pretty cool," Joe said. "So do you design your mazes up here too?" He glanced at the papers lying on the table.

Alan quickly gathered up the papers and shoved them into a deep drawer in the table. "Sometimes," he said abruptly, "but these aren't for anyone else's eyes just yet."

"I'm surprised you don't keep the doors locked, Alan," Joe said. "Frank and I were both able to just walk right in."

"I keep all the doors leading into here locked," Alan said, his tone harsh. "When I'm not here, they're locked. Once in a while, when I'm up here,

I don't lock the doors—but Penny and the twins don't invade my little den unless they're invited."

"I hear you," Joe said. "And Frank and I wouldn't have, either, if we'd known what was up here. But we're on the case now, so don't be surprised if we show up in some unexpected places. We're determined to help you find out who's trying to destroy your maze. And that means following up on *anything* we think seems suspicious."

"Good," Alan said. The harshness in his voice had softened a little. "I appreciate it."

"Speaking of suspicious, the twins told me about Vincenzo Blackstone."

Alan's expression turned dark again as he frowned and jutted out his chin in a defiant angle. "That reprobate!" he said. "I'll be surprised if he's *not* behind the problems we had yesterday. He has no qualms about destroying other people's property or lives. I've already put out a few feelers among some friends to see if they know he's behind the trouble. I called Officer Chester this morning, and the police are on it too. I'll bet you anything Blackstone will turn up on the island. And if he does, I'm sure he's planning more trouble."

"Frank and I are trying to figure out how the archer lit his arrow without attracting some attention. An obvious way would have been for him to use the fire-eater's equipment. Frank talked to him and he seemed okay, but we wanted to check with you. Do you know him personally, or did you hire him just for this event?"

"I don't know him at all," Alan said, "but I think he's from Newfoundland. I hired him through a talent agency in Halifax. I can give you the name and number of the person I talked to there." He jotted a few notes on a small scrap of paper. He handed Joe the paper, then walked to a large trunk that served as a table next to the reading chair. "Would you like to see the gauntlet?"

"Oh, yeah," Joe said eagerly, joining Alan at the trunk.

With a flourish, Alan lifted the heavy lid and reached inside. Joe peered into the deep cavity of the trunk . . . and saw nothing.

5 Pay the Piper

Alan didn't speak for a minute. He just stared into the empty trunk. Then he closed the lid.

"You know," he said, "I just remembered. I told Penny to put it in the safe in our closet." He nodded his head. "Yeah, that's where I told her to put it, and I'm sure she did just that."

He beamed a big smile at Joe. "Well, you'd better be getting out to the stables," he said. "Shorty is waiting for you. He'll put you through your paces with Abiyad so you'll be ready for the amateur jousting matches."

"Are there any more entrances into this room?" Joe asked.

"Sure," Alan said. "All of the secret rooms in this house have more than one escape route."

Joe looked around the room, trying to figure out where the other exit was. "So where—"

A ringing phone interrupted his question. Alan opened a drawer in the long table and pulled out a phone, but he didn't answer it. Instead, he turned to Joe and smiled. "Better get going," he said. "You need to log some practice time if you're going to get that brass ring."

The phone kept ringing, but Alan waited until Joe walked toward the door. As Joe walked down the narrow staircase, he heard Alan pick up the phone and whisper a few words, but he couldn't make out what was said. Joe lingered halfway down the staircase before Alan firmly closed the door behind him.

Joe tried to hear anything through the door, but he couldn't—so he left the house and headed for the bazaar.

He heard Kay's laughter first, then spotted her talking to a boot maker who was working in one of the booths. "Joe, look!" she called when she saw him walking up. She turned her leg around in both directions. "What do you think?" White leather boots were pulled up over her jeans and turned down into cuffs above her knees.

"They're perfect," Joe assured her. "Just what you need for a medieval adventure."

"I totally agree," she said, peeling them off. While the boot maker continued to measure her feet and legs for her custom-made pair of boots, Joe asked Kay about the couple he wanted to interview.

"Officer Chester pointed them out to me last night," he said. "They were helping you clean out the burned hedge. The officer said they lived in the village, and they saw someone running toward the forest at about the same time I did. I'd like to talk to them and compare notes."

"You must mean JoAnne and Harold Donaldson," Kay said. "I saw them over near the food vendors just before I came here. They were in line then, so they're probably still eating."

"Great," Joe said. "Maybe I can catch them before they move on. See you later."

Joe left Kay with the boot maker and headed toward the large tents where the caterers served food. He saw the Donaldsons sitting alone at a large table near the edge of the tent. He grabbed a soda and joined them.

"Welcome," JoAnne Donaldson said. She was wearing a blue satin dress with billowing sleeves and eating a bowl of salad with blueberries.

Joe introduced himself and told them why he wanted to talk to them.

"We already told Officer Chester what we saw," JoAnne said.

"Yes, he told me," Joe explained. "I saw someone running into the woods at about the same time. I

43

just wanted to compare pictures with you and see if we're talking about the same guy."

"Well, he was about six feet, two or three inches," Harold Donaldson said, putting down his turkey drumstick. He wore a hunter green fencing vest. A fencer's mesh helmet lay on the table next to a plate of cheeses. "He was a big guy," Harold added. "Stocky and thick, you know?"

"What was he wearing?" Joe asked.

"Some kind of costume," JoAnne answered. "Armor or chain mail, something like that. He had on a helmet or hood—we couldn't really see his face or his hair."

"Yeah, that's about what I saw, too," Joe said. "Was he carrying anything—an archer's bow or a crossbow?"

"I didn't see anything like that. Did you, Harold?" JoAnne asked her husband.

"No, come to think of it, he wasn't carrying anything," Harold said. "I'm afraid we're not a lot of help."

"Well, at least we know we all saw the same guy," Joe said.

"It's a terrible thing for Alan," JoAnne added. "He's been working so long on that maze."

"And he's determined to get it open in a day or two," Joe assured them as he stood to leave. "Thanks for your time."

❖ ❖ ❖ ❖

While Joe was talking with Alan and then the Donaldsons, Frank and Ray milled through the bazaar, asking specific vendors if they'd seen or heard from Vincenzo Blackstone.

After a couple of hours of negative responses, Ray left to help his dad in the stadium, and Frank headed toward the stables. When he arrived, the only other person there was a man walking one of the horses around a small ring. Frank introduced himself.

"They told me you'd be coming by for a mount," the man said. "I'm Shorty Garber, the trainer hereabouts. This here's your horse, Abiyad."

"Man, he's great!" Frank said. The horse was large and coal black, with huge eyes that stared right into Frank's. "He's a real beauty."

"Aye, that he is," Shorty said. "And a champion at the games too. He'll give you a good ride."

Frank peeled off his jacket, and Shorty gave him a boost up into the saddle. Frank adjusted his seat and trotted the large horse around the ring a few times. Then Shorty handed him a jousting lance.

The Hardys had been to medieval fairs before and had even held jousting lances. Still, Frank was struck by how clumsy the wooden pole felt as he perched atop Abiyad. The lance was about ten feet long and tapered down to a rounded end in the front. The back end was much thicker and heavier, and it took him a few minutes to adjust to the weight and balance as he grasped it.

"The trick is to hold it straight," Shorty told him. "Make sure it's parallel to the ground. If it dips down—in front or back—it'll throw your balance off and maybe drag you down with it. And it'll be harder for the horse to keep his footing too."

Shorty helped support the lance while Frank grasped it in one hand. After a few minutes, Frank found the exact place to clamp down on the shaft so that the weight was balanced and the lance was straight and horizontal. He clicked the horse back into a slow walk around the ring, and concentrated on balancing the lance. After a few more minutes he urged Abiyad into a trot, and then a canter. Most of the time he was able to hold the lance straight.

Finally, he took a few passes at a hoop hanging from a scaffolding at the end of the ring. It took him seven tries, but he finally managed to snag the hoop onto the front end of the jousting lance.

"Nice going!" Joe yelled from the side of the ring as Frank rode over to meet him. Joe was on a creamy white horse, cradling his jousting lance in the crook of his elbow.

Frank pulled up and lowered the thick end of the lance to the ground. He was sweating and winded, but he felt great.

"I'm sorry I didn't get here sooner," Joe said. "I got sidetracked with Alan." He told Frank about his meeting in the hidden room.

"And Alan was okay with the gauntlet not being in the trunk?" Frank asked.

"He was pretty weird about it at first, but then he said he remembered where it was. He acted really strangely about the phone call, though. He let it ring until I left before he answered it. And I remembered something else. The phone didn't have any dialing mechanism—just two buttons."

"Too bad you didn't hear more of his conversation," Frank said.

"I know," Joe agreed. "When I finally got out of there, I went to the bazaar and found JoAnne and Harold Donaldson." He reported what they had told him about the person running into the woods.

"I didn't have nearly as much luck," Frank said. "No one's seen Vincenzo Blackstone. No one's heard from him in a while. No one knows whether he was planning to show up here. No one knows where he is now. It's like he's totally disappeared."

"Or in hiding, maybe," Joe said. "Lying low while he plots his next move on Alan's maze."

"Maybe," Frank said. "Remember, Kay told us that when he destroyed that other maze, he hired some guys to do the dirty work. If he's done that here, maybe something will leak out. We need to stay on it—keep bringing it up with everyone we talk to."

"Meanwhile, we've got about an hour to get into shape for these amateur games." Joe reached down to pat the sleek neck of his creamy white horse. "Come on, Khayyam," he said, balancing his jousting lance. "Show me what you can do."

The Hardys practiced for another fifty-five minutes, until they both reached a point when they were able to catch the hoop more times than they missed it. When he heard the cannon announcing the "Call to the Games," Frank felt pumped. And he could tell from the familiar look in Joe's eyes that he was ready to compete too.

"You two go on over to the stadium and get registered," Shorty told them. "We'll bring the horses by later."

The stands were already filled with an exuberant crowd. Brass rings—the jousting targets—dangled and twirled from scaffolding and shot sunlit rays around the field. Heraldic flags and pennants streamed down from the scaffold end posts, adding their own vibrant colors to the scene.

Alan and Penny sat astride their horses at the far end of the stadium. Alan was outfitted in full jousting regalia, and Penny was dressed like a medieval queen in a long purple gown. In front of them stood a bagpiper flanked by two drummers. Each of the musicians was dressed in full heraldic regalia, complete with boots and helmets with long visors to shade their faces from the afternoon sun.

Frank and Joe checked in at the competitors'

registration table, and then joined Ray and Kay on the sidelines.

"Looks like we're going to have a full house after all," Kay said. "Mom was right. It'll take more than sparks from a flaming arrow to scare off this wild crowd."

The chatter of the spectators quieted as the piper blew a few practice notes. The only other sounds were flags flapping in the sea breeze, and the snorts and whinnys from the holding pen behind the stands.

The piper began playing an old Scottish march, "Robert Bruce's March to Bannockburn." Alan and Penny rode slowly behind, as the drummers held a steady beat.

Frank moved away from his brother and the twins so that he could get a better view. When the mini-parade reached the end of the field, Alan and Penny turned their horses around to face the spectators. The musicians left the field, the drummers to the left and the piper to the right toward Frank.

Frank watched as the man unbuckled his bagpipe and dropped it on the ground. Without looking back, the piper hurried around the corner of the stands in the direction of the horse pen.

"Hey, Joe," Frank called over the heads of other onlookers. "Did you see that?" It was obvious that Joe didn't hear him. He and the twins had moved farther down the sidelines. Alan's voice poured from the loudspeakers as he welcomed the crowd, but Frank just stared at the expensive bagpipe sitting in the dirt. "Something's up," he mumbled to himself. "No musician just dumps his instrument like that."

Frank picked up the bagpipe and started to follow the piper's path behind the stands. As he rounded the corner, he felt the ground vibrating beneath his boots. The pounding thunder coming toward him drowned out all other noise.

Storming straight at him was Abiyad, panting and stomping at full speed. Atop him sat the piper, his black eyes glaring ahead beneath the silver helmet visor. A jousting lance swayed from his clenched fist.

"Hiyah! Hiyah!" The fury of Abiyad's gallop was urged on by his rider's shouts. Frank was so stunned by the sight of the huge horse that he couldn't move at first. He couldn't even think.

A glob of Abiyad's drool flung onto Frank's cheek. Like a light punch, it kick-started his mind and body back into action. With one powerful surge, Frank vaulted into the air.

6 Vanished!

Still holding the bagpipe, Frank leaped to the right and out of Abiyad's path. The horse and rider barreled past him as Frank landed with a wheezing groaning sound—half Frank, half bagpipe.

Shaking his head to clear his mind after the hard landing, he watched Abiyad roar toward the stadium entrance, mane flying and hooves flinging sod in all directions. The piper pointed the jousting lance straight ahead, holding it.

Frank started to run after them, but then doubled back into the horse's pen and grabbed Khayyam's reins from Shorty's hand. He swung up into the saddle and urged the horse toward the stadium.

He reached the entrance in less than a minute. Alan had finished his speech, and Penny began walking their horses back up the field. The piper entered the field and bolted after them, his lance aimed forward.

At first the crowd cheered and whooped, thinking the man on the black horse was part of the show. When Frank flew onto the field on Khayyam, the spectators rose to their feet in an even greater wave of excitement.

"Alan!" Frank yelled. "Behind you!" At first, he couldn't be heard over the cheers. He urged Khayyam to a faster gallop.

Out of the corner of his eye, he saw some of the people in the stands point and yell. The crowd noise quickly died down, and a couple of screams pierced the air.

"Alan!" Frank called again. "Heads up!"

This time, Alan heard Frank. And so did the piper.

Alan and Penny wheeled their horses around. When they saw the man bearing down on them, they split, galloping off to opposite sides of the ring.

When he heard Frank's call, the piper whipped his head around. He lost his hold on the lance, and his bulky body dipped way down to the left. Abiyad pulled up and skidded to a sudden, hoof-clattering halt. He reared back up and lifted his powerful forelegs high into the air. The rider slid out of the saddle and slammed to the ground. The piper's head hit the ground so hard that his helmet bounced off and a bushy shock of red hair and beard tumbled out.

Frank pulled Khayyam to a stop and tumbled from the saddle as an explosion of whistles and yells burst from the stands. He raced toward the fallen piper, kicking the man's lance away from the action.

The piper rolled his body into a standing position, but he seemed unsteady as he wiped the dirt off his arms and legs. Then he appeared to get his bearings again as he looked at Frank. His glare drilled into Frank's eyes.

"Bruce David MacLaren!" Alan yelled, stomping up behind Frank. Joe and Ray joined them from the sidelines. "Get off my property. You're not welcome here!"

"You'll not tell me what to do," MacLaren bellowed. His bushy auburn beard bristled as he spoke.

"I will on my own property," Alan thundered back. "How did you get in here, anyway?"

"It's amazing how much these old costumes can hide, isn't it?" MacLaren said with a sneer. "They make a perfect disguise."

As Frank watched the two men, Shorty pulled up in an all-terrain vehicle. Next to him sat one of the security guards Alan had hired for the tournament.

"Well, your cover is blown now, and you're not welcome on my land!" Alan repeated. "Ever! You're through making trouble for me and my family."

Alan turned to the ATV. "Shorty, get him out of here," he ordered.

MacLaren took a step forward. Then he looked from Alan to Frank and back to Alan. He backed up and glared for a few more seconds. "This is not over, Chezleigh Alan Horton," he finally snarled. "I know it . . . and you know it too." Then he spat on the ground as a final insult and stomped away toward the exit.

Alan nodded to Shorty, and the trainer guided the vehicle slowly behind MacLaren as he marched across the field. The spectators booed and yelled at the man being thrown out of the party. MacLaren pumped his fist at the crowd in a dramatic gesture of defiance.

"We'll take the horses back to the pen," Frank offered. "They need cooling down." Alan nodded to them with a grim half smile. Then he waved to the crowd and walked to the microphone.

As the Hardys and Ray walked Abiyad and Khayyam off the field, Alan assured the crowd that the excitement had only just begun. "Just a little preview of the thrills in store for us all," he said. "Didn't I tell you this tournament would be fantastic?" The crowd responded with more cheers and whistles.

"Dad's great, isn't he?" Ray said as he walked with the Hardys. "Nothing seems to get him down for long." In spite of his friend's positive words, Frank could see that he was worried.

"He's totally cool," Joe agreed. "But what's the story behind this MacLaren jerk? Obviously you guys have had problems with him before. Is he another Mazemaster competitor?"

"No, but he's been trying to get my dad in trouble for years," Ray said. "Dad has this fantastic collection of medieval paraphernalia and artifacts, and MacLaren's jealous, that's all. Plus, he's accused Dad of purchasing some of the pieces from unscrupulous dealers."

"Meaning that the sellers were selling stolen goods?" Frank guessed.

"That's what MacLaren claimed," Ray acknowledged. "He says the pieces were stolen from museums and private owners and then sold to Dad and other collectors."

"And he thinks your dad knows the stuff is stolen property?"

"Yes," Ray admitted. "But it's not true, of course. My dad has always sworn that every purchase has been legal by international law and by the laws of each item's original country."

"He should be able to prove that if anyone has any doubt," Joe pointed out.

"And he can," Ray said. "He's got full documentation on everything."

"That should be enough to satisfy MacLaren," Frank said. "What's his problem?"

"He claims the documents and receipts are all

fake," Ray answered. "His father used to make the same claims against my grandfather. Bruce MacLaren insists that our family is responsible for removing historical artifacts from his country, chiefly from his family. But the real truth is that MacLaren's ancestors were thieves and pirates. Nearly everything they ever had of value was stolen by them to begin with. In the last century, a lot of their stuff was sold off to pay attorney fees to keep them out of prison and to pay off gambling debts. Bruce MacLaren himself has quite a reputation around the casinos of Europe."

"Sounds like the bad blood between your family and MacLaren goes back for quite a while," Joe commented.

"Yeah, but we can handle it," Ray said, his jaw so tight that Joe could see a muscle tremor. "He sued us last year, but the judge threw out the case."

As they neared the pen, Frank spotted the bagpipe. He felt a twinge in his hip as he remembered leaping out of Abiyad's path. He reached down and picked up the instrument. As he examined it, he told Joe and Ray about chasing after MacLaren earlier.

"One of these pipes is cracked," he said, looking at the bagpipe. "No big surprise. Hmmm, look at this." He wet his thumb and rubbed the side of the mouthpipe.

Joe and Ray looked closely at the place Frank

pointed to. "It's a *B*," Ray said, "in Old English script, like the one on the arrow shaft you found."

Frank rubbed off more of the wet dirt that had packed against the mouthpipe. "Here's a *D* and an *M*," he said.

"Bruce David MacLaren," Ray said.

"Looks like it's definitely his," Joe agreed. "Bagpipes are expensive—and musicians are usually so careful with their instruments. It's pretty amazing that he'd just throw it away like that."

"Yeah," Ray said, nodding. "And this is the guy who's supposed to be so interested in preserving artifacts and family treasures. I told you he's a liar. I can't believe he was able to get in here. And I wonder what happened to the piper we hired."

"We'd better check that out," Joe said. "MacLaren seems pretty vicious. No telling what he might have done to keep the regular piper off the field."

"Could MacLaren have been the guy you saw running into the woods after the flaming arrow hit its mark, Joe?" Frank asked.

"It's hard to say exactly, because he was so far away, but he could have been," Joe answered. "He's about the same size."

"Does your dad still have the arrow shaft?" Frank asked Ray. "I'd like to have Officer Chester see it."

"I saw him put it in his desk in the library," Ray answered. "We can check it out when we get back to the house."

"So far, MacLaren has gone after your father through the legal system. But that scene on the field was different."

"Frank's right, Ray," Joe said. "It might have all been an act, but it looked like he was going after your folks with that lance. Who knows what might have happened if Frank hadn't stopped him."

"And shooting fire over a crowd of people was a really risky move," Frank pointed out. "If Bruce MacLaren was the archer, the dispute between him and your dad may have escalated to a new and dangerous level."

After Abiyad had rested, Frank and Joe entered the jousting competition. A natural athlete and a practiced horseman, Joe got better with each heat, ultimately eliminating everyone else and taking home the prize for his division of amateur jousters.

Riding Khayyam, Frank came in fourth, so dinner that evening with their hosts and the other winners was a celebration. Joe's prize was an authentic burgonet, a lightweight steel helmet once worn by Scottish highlanders. One of the most popular helmets of the sixteenth century, it had a long, wide visor but was very open in front, offering plenty of fresh air for the long rides. Frank won a leather belt with a dragonhead buckle.

After dinner, Alan and Ray went to the maze to

oversee the repairs, and Penny and Kay ran the evening games in the stadium.

Frank and Joe divided their time between being spectators and investigators. They split up and canvassed all the vendors for news of Vincenzo Blackstone. Several said they wouldn't be surprised to find out that he was on the island, but no one admitted to actually seeing him.

Frank also checked with Shorty, who reported that the original piper had shown up claiming to have been knocked out and tied up by someone. "Frankly, I don't believe him," Shorty confided. "I've got a feeling he was paid off by MacLaren to stay out of the way."

Joe checked in with Skip Jennin at the film studio, who said the Hardys could come in any time on Sunday and view all the footage they wanted.

When the Hardys finally hit the sheets that night, they agreed that they knew more than they had the night before. But their investigation had rustled up a new twist—in the shape of a red-headed piper.

"Joe! Frank! Wake up!" Kay's frantic voice jolted Joe to an instant alert. He sat straight up in his bed and shook the Saturday night sleep out of his brain.

"Joe!" Kay's voice called again from the other side of the door. "Oh, please wake up." The sound of a pounding fist against the old wooden door got him out of bed.

"Coming," he called back. "Just a minute." He pulled on his jeans and headed for the door, punching Frank's shoulder along the way. "Let's go, Frank. It sounds like trouble."

When Joe opened the door, Kay was already in the middle of a sentence.

"—and then we finally realized," she said. Her voice was loud and her words were fast. "We can't figure out what happened! There's nothing, no clue. You've got to help us!"

"Slow down," Frank said gently as he joined Joe at the door. "Of course we'll help. What happened?"

"It's Dad," Kay said. Her glance darted from Joe to Frank and back to Joe again. Her voice was suddenly soft and shaky, as if she were trying to swallow her words. "He's disappeared!"

7 Which Way to China?

"You don't know where your dad is?" Joe asked. "Have you checked the maze? the stables? that secret study upstairs?"

"No, it's not like that," Kay insisted. "He's really gone. I'm afraid something's happened to him. I just know it. Come downstairs—Mom and Ray are in the sunroom."

"Okay," Frank said. "Let us get cleaned up. We'll be down in a minute."

The Hardys cleaned up, pulled on fresh jeans and sweaters, and were in the sunroom in minutes.

"Hey man, thanks," Ray said, clapping Frank on the back as he walked in. "This is really serious. I'm glad you guys are here."

"We are too," Frank assured him. "Okay, what's going on?"

"Mom, tell them about last night," Kay urged.

"Well, I got a headache during the last jousting match and came back to the house early," Penny said. She rubbed her head while she talked, and her hand trembled.

"I had some tea and toast, took some medicine, and went to bed," Penny continued. "I didn't hear any of you come in—I was really out, I guess." She got up and walked over to the window. The sun shot long streaks of warm light across the marble floor.

"When I woke up this morning, I realized that Alan had never come into the room during the night," she concluded, turning back away from the window. "His side of the bed was undisturbed. The clothes he'd worn last night were missing. His wallet and cell phone were not on the dresser—but he always puts them there when he goes to bed."

Penny looked at the twins. "He's gone," she said simply. "Just gone. I've called his cell phone a dozen times and always get the voice mail. I've left a message each time, but he hasn't called back."

"But that doesn't necessarily mean something's happened to him," Frank said. He tried to keep his voice calm and assuring. Penny looked as if she was barely controlling her feelings and might break down any minute.

"Isn't it possible that he's just working some-where on the grounds and forgot to check in?" Joe asked. "Maybe he left his cell phone off and just hasn't picked up the messages yet. He's doing everything he can to get the maze opening back on schedule. Maybe he started working out there and didn't feel like stopping."

"That's the first place I looked," Ray said. "He's not there, and there's no sign that he was there last night."

"There's a half-eaten sandwich in here," Kay said. She led the others into the kitchen and showed them the plate on the extra-long wooden table that ran down the center of the huge room. "And this is his mug—there's some coffee still in it. But I don't know whether it's from last night or this morning."

"We've called all over the estate," Ray told the Hardys. "Shorty's apartment is above the stables. He said Dad wasn't out there last night, and the horses are all accounted for."

"None of the security people saw him," Kay said.

"We've got fifteen vehicles altogether," Ray added. "Three cars, three trucks, two tractors, four golf carts, one motorcycle, and two ATVs. They're all here, all parked where they should be."

"We've got lots of bikes, and they're all out there too," Kay pointed out.

"The scary thing is that there's no note, no phone

call," Penny said quietly. She poured coffee for everyone and passed around a tin of raisin scones. "He always calls or leaves a note if he's going to be late or gets tied up somewhere," she added.

Frank took a swig of hot coffee. "Okay," he said. "He's out there somewhere. Let's find him. Penny, you take another look through the maze. No offense, Ray, but it pays to double-check each place. Kay, go over everything. Look for new damage, any branches that have been broken since the mess from the night before last."

"And check the security shed," Joe told them. "See if everything looks normal there. If someone got in the maze last night, he or she would have to disarm the security system."

"Okay," Kay said. "What are you guys going to do?"

"We'll check around the estate again and make some calls to people in the village," Frank answered. "Is there a landscaper we can call, for instance? Where would your dad go to get replacement hedges for the maze? We can also check with taxi services. We'll call the police, too, and see if your dad's reported anything about his confrontation with Bruce MacLaren."

"Take your cell phone," Joe told Kay. "Call right away if you find anything."

Kay and Penny left for the maze, and the Hardys and Ray went right to work. Frank asked Ray to check with the local landscapers, gardeners, and taxi services.

"We don't actually have any real cab companies," Ray said. "But there is one guy in the village who will drive people places for a fee."

"Close enough," Joe said. "See if your dad contacted him last night."

"Or if he saw your dad at all," Frank added.

"Do you want me to call the police, too?" Ray asked.

"That's probably a good idea," Frank said. "You might get more out of them than an outsider would."

While Ray made the calls from the library, Joe and Frank set out on their search of the house. The first place they went was Alan's secret study. The hidden door in the back of the closet was locked, but with a few twists of Frank's lockpick, they were in. They jogged up the stairs into Alan's retreat.

There were no clues as to his whereabouts, but because of Alan's disappearance, the brothers had no qualms about giving the place a thorough once-over. Frank was especially interested in the room because he had been stopped by Alan before actually getting inside. Joe turned on the light and small fan hanging over the long table.

"Any thoughts on what's going on with Alan?" Joe asked his brother.

"No, not really. But it doesn't look good."

"Yeah, that's what I'm thinking too."

"In the last two days he's been threatened anonymously with a flaming arrow, his maze has been vandalized, and he's been nearly attacked by Bruce MacLaren," Frank summed up.

"And don't forget the phone call I almost overheard," Joe said, opening another drawer. "Empty. The phone's gone too."

"We need to find him, Joe. Soon."

"He had these strange papers out when I was here before," Joe said, walking over to the drawing table that stretched along one wall. "They were like diagrams or schematics."

"Maybe his maze plans?" Frank guessed.

"That's what I thought," Joe said. "But he never confirmed that. In fact"—Joe opened one of the wide drawers in the table—"he dumped them into this drawer before I got a really good look at them. Said they weren't for anyone else's eyes, or something like that."

Joe pulled the drawer all the way out, but it was empty. Then he went to the trunk where Alan had said the golden gauntlet was being kept. It was unlocked. Joe lifted the lid, and the trunk was still empty.

"Looks like this room has been cleaned out," Joe murmured.

"Not entirely," Frank said. He had opened the

second wide drawer in the drawing table. I found this stuck in the back corner of this drawer." He showed Joe a crumpled fragment of paper, which he smoothed into a wrinkled rectangle on the tabletop. The page was divided into curved bands. Each band contained short black lines in various groupings. Some lines were used as the four sides of a square, some formed an L-shape, and some just stood vertically by themselves.

"Could be a maze design," Joe said. "If we had the whole piece of paper, these arcs could be parts of circles within circles, like in a maze. And the lines in the circles could indicate where the paths would lead to dead ends, or where they would lead to the center of the maze."

Frank nodded. He smoothed and folded the piece of paper and put it in his pocket. The Hardys finished their search of the secret study, but found nothing to indicate where Alan might be.

They continued checking the rest of the house, including doors and windows, but found no clues. Finally, they rejoined Ray in the library.

"I've got nothing," Ray said, slumping back in the large leather wing chair at the library desk. "Nobody's seen or talked to Dad since the end of the jousting matches last night."

Frank pulled out the piece of paper. "Do you know what this is?" he asked.

"That looks like some of the designs I've seen

Dad working on," Ray answered. "He doodles that stuff all the time—I figure it's for a maze."

"That's what we thought too," Joe said, as Frank put the paper back into his pocket. "Have you seen the golden gauntlet since your mom brought it back to the house Friday night?"

"No, why?" Ray answered.

"Your dad was going to show it to me in a trunk in his secret study, but it wasn't there. He acted kind of funny about it, but said he'd told your mom to put it somewhere else. Check with her on that when they call in, okay?"

"They called a few minutes ago," Ray answered. "Kay said the security shed at the maze looked okay, and the alarm system was activated. I'll ask about the gauntlet the next time they call."

"Okay, let's go," Frank said. "It's time to check the rest of the estate."

"What are we looking for?" Ray said. "We've got one hundred eighty acres. All the vehicles are parked. You don't think he's out somewhere on foot, do you?"

"Probably not," Frank conceded. "But I'm not ready to rule it out." He exchanged glances with Joe and knew that his brother was having the same thoughts. Although it was unlikely Alan was out there walking around, he could still be out there without wheels—and he might need help.

Ray led them to the vehicle shed. He and Frank

took one ATV, and Joe drove the other. Frank reported their plan to Penny and Kay, who were still making a painstaking tour of the enormous maze. Penny told him she'd put the gauntlet in the secret study trunk, and hadn't seen it since.

The Hardys and Ray first checked all the out-buildings, but they yielded nothing—nor did exploration of the stables, the stadium, or the medieval bazaar. The latter was already full of customers even though the vendors were just beginning to set up.

The grounds of EagleSpy included hills, valleys, meadows, gardens, the shore along Golden Arm Lake, a waterfall and brook, and a small forest. As the boys raced across the property, Ray reached under the seat and pulled out a hunter's horn. He periodically blew the Horton family distress call, but there was no answering call.

"Oh man, I've got to stop and walk for a few minutes," Ray finally declared. He seemed really stressed. Frank knew exactly how it felt to be searching for a missing father. He and Joe had been there, and it wasn't pleasant.

Frank gestured to Joe, and they both stopped the ATVs near a small hill. Ray jumped out of the passenger side and just ran off without a word. Then he broke into a sprint and raced to a distant tree. He turned around and raced back, then started a second loop. Joe crouched a few times, did some calf stretches, and began running the same laps.

Frank knew how the other boys felt. It was great to straighten his knees and get out of the cramped ATV. He took a few deep breaths and was surprised that he tasted salt in the air. *Golden Arm Lake must be nearby,* he reasoned, and started a steady trot in the direction his nose led him. He loped along about fifty yards to the hill, then turned and began circling around its base.

The air was even more pungent on the other side of the hill, so he decided to keep going. After a few more yards, he noticed a strange sensation in his feet. At first he thought his ankles were giving way, but then he realized it was the ground: It seemed spongy and uneven, although it looked perfectly level.

Frank slowed his trot to a walk. "The ground must be wet here," he mumbled to no one. "Maybe it's sandy or something. Like I'm close to the lakeshore or a bea . . . eee . . . no . . . nooooo!"

In an instant, the ground beneath him gave way completely, and he plunged straight down into the earth.

8 Hack, You're It

"Frank!" Joe called, as he and Ray walked up the small hill. "Frank! Where are you?"

It seemed like a crazy question, because the land was clear and open on the other side of the hill. There appeared to be no place for Frank to hide.

"The mine!" Ray yelled. "Frank! Frank!" He tried to blow the hunter's horn, but nothing came out but sputters and spits.

"What mine?" Joe called over to Ray. "What are you talking about?"

"Don't move," Ray warned. "Just stand still for a minute." Ray took a few tentative half steps, tapping his toe on the ground. "Frank? Can you hear me?"

"Yeah, I'm over here." Frank's voice sounded far

away and hollow. His words were repeated in a low echo.

"Hey man, you okay?" Joe called.

"I think so," Frank's voice returned from a spot about twenty yards away. Joe could barely make out a large patch of fresh brown dirt in the middle of the bright green grass. "I fell into some kind of tunnel. I can see a little with the light from the opening I fell through. Just a minute, let me get my flashlight on."

There was silence for a minute or two, then Frank's voice sounded again in that hollow echo. "I'm about ten feet down, I guess," he said. "There's some wood framing along the walls. I think I'm in some kind of mine."

"It's a marble mine," Ray yelled to him. "It crisscrosses under the whole estate. Can you see very far into it?"

"I can," Frank said. "I've got my pocket flash on and I can see ahead about thirty yards. I can tell from your voices that I'm facing in your direction. There's nothing but wall behind me and on both sides."

"I'm afraid for us to come over to you," Ray said. He and Joe stood about twenty yards away. "If the ground gives under us, it could cave in on you."

"Absolutely," Frank said. "Just stay where you are. I'm going to walk along the tunnel. It looks like there's some kind of pale light farther along. Maybe it widens out there, or there's another sinkhole in the ground."

"If you're facing us, you're looking toward the lake. The hill slopes down in that direction," Ray said. "There might be an opening to the mine tunnel there."

"Okay," Frank called out. "Here I go. If this doesn't work, I'll come back to this spot, and we'll try something else."

"Oh man, I don't like this," Joe muttered. "Be careful," he called out louder. "If it looks even a little weird, come back."

"Don't worry, I will," Frank answered. "Okay, here I go," he repeated. Then there was silence.

Joe squinted at the dark area where the ground had swallowed Frank. "I can't just stand here," he told Ray. "I have to do something."

"Okay," Ray said. "See that bunch of birch trees over there?"

Joe followed Ray's pointing finger and saw a couple dozen thin, straight trees with white and pale gray bark striped with occasional bands of black. The trees shot up from a thick mass of green weeds and undergrowth, but he caught an occasional glimpse of blue glinting through the tangled leaves and twigs.

"The lakeshore is on the other side of those birches," Ray said. "That's the direction Frank is walking—that's where he said the pale light was coming from. Go see if you can find an entrance to the mine tunnel around there. I'll stay here in case Frank has to turn back."

Slowly, cautiously, Joe stepped down the hill and walked toward the lake.

Ten feet belowground, Frank's flashlight shot a wide, steady beam. Each time the light hit a dark patch of dirt, something slithered or scampered back into the shadows. There was a peculiar smell, almost metallic, and a gritty gray dust bounced in the beam of light.

Frank's eyes adjusted to the harsh contrast of light and dark as he walked. He tuned his ears to every sound, ignoring the skitters and rustles and listening instead for the more perilous cracking and creaking of the walls that would signal a cave-in. *I can handle the things that live down here,* he told himself, *but I'm not ready to become a permanent resident myself.*

Every once in a while he swung the beam of light to the ground and squinted ahead. He still saw that pale glow, and each time, it was a little nearer. Finally he grew close enough to see that the glow was formed by individual patches of light piercing through tiny openings.

At last, he came to the source of the glow. A few rotted boards marked what had apparently once been an opening to the outside. The powdery wood

74

had been plastered with a tangle of weeds and vines, which allowed hundreds of pinpoints of light to poke through.

Frank pocketed his flashlight and began tearing away at the branches and vines.

"Frank!" Joe called from the other side. "Hey!"

The two of them tore away at the barrier until Frank could step through. The sunlight blinded him for a minute as it ricocheted off the rocking waves of the lake.

The brothers clamped arms, and both took a deep breath.

"You made it!" Ray called, running over to join them.

Frank brushed a few slugs and beetles out of his hair with an involuntary shudder. "Okay, it's time to go back to work," he said. "Do you suppose your father could have fallen into a tunnel the way I did?" he asked, turning to Ray.

"I don't think so," Ray said. "I sure hope not. You're the first person who's fallen in that I know of since the mine's been closed. There was a terrible cave-in eighty years ago, which prompted it to be shut down for good."

"Is it just abandoned?" Frank asked. "Who owns it?"

"We do, now," Ray said. "But Dad has no intention of ever opening it up again. The locals talk about a curse connected with it. Supposedly there are still miners' bodies down there, and anyone who disturbs the mine takes on the curse. Dad sealed up all the entrances that were marked on the mine map over five years ago when we first moved here. I don't remember seeing this one on the map, though."

"Well, I'm sure glad it was here," Joe said.

"Dad's going to be pretty upset when he finds out about this," Ray told Frank. "You could have really been hurt."

"I'm okay," Frank said. "We probably should rope off this area just in case anyone else is wandering around over here."

"You're right," Ray agreed. "It's pretty isolated over here, but you never know. . . ."

"Have you got anything on the ATVs that we can use?" Frank asked. "Rope or chains, something like that?"

"Each one has a chain, but there's not enough to cordon off this area. There's an old caretaker's cottage down the beach, and I bet there's some rope there."

"You two go get it," Frank said. "I'll stay here. I can check in with your sister and try your dad's cell phone again while I wait."

Joe and Frank started down the beach. The sandy shore was very narrow and littered with large hunks of driftwood. A couple of times, the tide washed over their cross-trainers.

After walking for about twenty minutes, they

rounded a jetty and saw a small house on a butte about fifteen feet up from the shore. They left the sand and hiked up the short path to the cottage.

"This place hasn't been used for fifty years," Ray explained. "A caretaker lived here. I think they launched sailboats from the end of the jetty."

"It's pretty impressive," Joe said, gazing out over the panoramic view. He saw nothing but shoreline laced with trees, the vast slate blue lake, and a few large islands far out in the water. As he watched, a bald eagle appeared from nowhere and surged into a powerful swoop toward a spindly pine tree. With an instantaneous switch of gears, it raised its huge shoulders and lowered its landing gear, grasping the treetop with killer claws.

"If I lived here," Joe said quietly, "this would be a very cool place to hang out."

The inside of the cottage was layered in dirt and sand, except for a few places where the wind had apparently blown through a broken window and swept the floor and furniture clear.

Joe's nose twitched as they walked around the two main rooms. "Are you sure no one's been here?" he asked.

"Sure . . . why?"

"I smell fish," Joe said, walking over to the kitchen.

"Yeah well, we're right next to a pretty big lake," Ray said with a grin.

"I smell *cooked* fish," Joe said. "Greasy cooked fish."

"I don't smell it," Ray said. "I don't smell anything but old dust and the lake. Maybe someone had a clambake on the beach nearby."

Joe poked around the kitchen, but didn't find any evidence of someone being there. He turned on a small stove burner, and the gas fire flamed up. "The stove is still connected to a gas line, did you know that?" Joe asked.

"Actually, no," Ray said, joining Joe in the kitchen. "I'll tell Dad."

"Speaking of your dad," Joe said, "let's get out of here and keep looking."

They grabbed a couple of coils of heavy rope and some tent spikes and hurried out of the cottage and back up to the beach where Frank was waiting.

The Hardys and Ray roped off a wide area around the sinkhole where Frank had fallen into the mine. They secured the ropes around the spikes and drove the wood into the ground with a couple of large rocks.

"Did you get hold of Kay?" Joe asked his brother as they pulled the rope tight.

"I did," Frank said. "They were back at the house. They found nothing at the maze, and there's still been no word from Alan."

"Did you tell them what happened here?" Ray asked.

"No—we can tell them when we get back," Frank said. "The police are on their way out to the house right now. They'll probably be there by the time we get back."

"I'm going to ask you guys not to mention this to the police until I get a chance to talk to Dad about it. This is private property, and I know Dad: He'll want to fix this himself—and probably haul in the contractors who were supposed to make that mine totally inaccessible in the first place. Dad's not going to want the whole village to know that the mine has been opened up."

"You mean because of the curse?" Joe asked. "That's crazy!"

"I'm sure it seems like that to you," Ray agreed. "But to a lot of people around here, the curse is very real. They are descendants of people who lost their lives in that mine. If Dad wants to tell everyone what happened, okay. But I'm not saying anything about it until I talk to him. And I'm asking you two to please keep quiet until then too."

Frank looked at Joe, and they both nodded. "Okay," Frank said. "It's your place—we'll do it your way."

The three walked back to the ATVs and headed inland. It took them forty-five minutes to get to the house, by which time Officer Chester had arrived. He, Kay, and Penny were talking in the sunroom. The officer remembered Joe from

Friday night, and Ray introduced him to Frank.

"Where have you been, Frank?" Kay asked. "You look like you've been digging in dirt!"

Everyone told the officer about the individual searches they had launched for Alan, and Joe asked him whether the police had figured out who the flaming arrow archer was.

"No," Officer Chester said. "But we're working on it."

"Did Dad get a chance to show you the arrow shaft that Frank found on the site?" Ray asked.

"No, I haven't heard anything about that," Officer Chester said. He had an odd way of speaking—very slow and deliberate. "Like to see it for myself, though."

"It's in Dad's desk in the library," Ray said. "I'll get it."

"Like to talk more about these fellas, too," Officer Chester said, checking his notebook, "Vincenzo Blackstone and Bruce David MacLaren. Like to know more about how they figure in with your family."

Penny and the Kay began talking at once, and Ray joined in when he returned with the arrow shaft. It was information Frank had already heard, so he gestured to Joe, and the Hardys quietly left the kitchen.

"I've got to get cleaned up," Frank said.

"I'll go with you," Joe said. "I want to copy the

stuff I pulled up about Blackstone and give it to Officer Chester."

Frank and Joe took the steps of the carved staircase two at a time. Inside the guest suite, Joe fired up his computer at the small table by the window while Frank took a quick shower.

Joe clicked into his private files and opened the folder labeled *Vincenzo Blackstone*. Inside was one file, named *VB*.

"Mmmmm, that's weird," he mumbled. "There should be four files in that folder." He clicked on *VB*, and the file opened onto the screen. There was only one page:

Hey, Joe Hardy
Think you're pretty smart?
Well, you're not even close.
Think you're a hacker?
You're nothing when it comes to fighting me.
Think you're a detective?
You're nothing when it comes to FINDING me.
Stay out of my computer.
Stay out of my business.
Or you'll be one sorry jouster.

9 Ring of Fire

Joe stared at the note for a few seconds. Then a spurt of adrenaline spurred him into action. He copied the file onto a CD and raced to Ray's room to print out the note. Then he grabbed the copies and charged back to the guest suite. Frank was ready in fresh jeans, sweater, and a jacket.

"Look at this." Joe showed Frank the note hacked into his computer. "This has to be from Blackstone," Joe reasoned. "It was in the folder I set up with his data. He traced my research back to my computer, hacked in, and left me this note."

"He knows your name," Frank pointed out.

"He got that from my own computer files."

"He knows you're a detective."

"He could have gotten that from my files, or

even from some article on the Internet about a past case that we cracked. And if he knows who I am, he knows who you are too," Joe pointed out.

"Here's the best part," Frank read. "He calls you a jouster. That means only one thing."

"That he was in the stadium last night," Joe said with a nod. "There's no reason to call me that otherwise."

"Or someone who works for him was here," Frank suggested, "and fed him a report."

"At this point, I'd bet anything that Blackstone's at least on the island."

"And his message is pretty clear," Frank said with a grim frown.

"Looks like Blackstone just moved to the top of the suspect list," Joe said, folding two copies of the note and sticking them in his sports bag.

"I agree," Frank said. "And let's not tell the family about this. They're already worried enough."

"Okay—let's get going. We need to get this investigation moving and find Alan."

The Hardys took the stairway two steps at a time again and skidded into the kitchen.

"Where's Officer Chester?" Joe asked.

"He left," Kay said. "He got a call to check out a fender bender in the village square."

"Why?" Ray asked. "Did you find out anything?"

"Uh, nothing . . . well . . . I have some information on Blackstone for him, that's all," Joe said.

"We'll take it to him when we go to the village," Frank said. "We're going in to see the rough cuts of the footage," he explained to the others.

"First, have some lunch," Penny urged. "It's been a hard morning, and it's already two o'clock. We have to keep healthy so we can find Alan."

Over a bowl of hearty soup, and sandwiches piled high with turkey and cheese, the Hardys and Ray told Kay and Penny about Frank's accident. Kay got maps of both the property and the mine, and laid them out on the big table.

"Here," Ray said, pointing to the spot where Frank disappeared. "This is where he fell through."

Frank and Joe both studied the maps, getting an idea of where the sinkhole was in relationship to the house, the stables, the maze, and the rest of the estate.

"And this must be the caretaker's cottage where you got the rope," Frank said, pointing to a small building located on the property map.

"That's it," Ray said. He told his family why he and Joe had gone to the cottage and how the three of them had roped off the sinkhole area.

"Ray said no one uses that cottage anymore," Joe said. "It's pretty cool—it would make a great beach party house."

"Someone might have already figured that out," Frank said. "Joe smelled cooked fish when he was in there. You may have some trespassers."

"It didn't look like anyone had been in the cabin," Ray said. "It was probably someone just using the beach for a bonfire cookout."

"We were in a hurry, though," Joe said. "We didn't get a chance to give it a thorough search."

"Sounds like it might need a second look," Frank said. He turned to Penny. "What's happening with the tournament today? Have you canceled any events, or is everything happening as scheduled?"

"Well, some of the events are on hold until the maze is repaired, and that might be as soon as this afternoon. But there's no way I can make the final inspection. Only Alan can declare it ready for the relays and the scavenger hunt competition."

"The medieval bazaar is really busy," Kay reported. "There were tons of people hitting all the booths and vendors, so that should keep things rolling out there for a while."

"We've got more competitions scheduled for the stadium this evening," Ray said, checking his watch. "I talked to Shorty before we started lunch, and he said everyone registered for the games has checked in. So we shouldn't cancel them."

"Can you three handle those without Alan?" Frank asked.

"And without our help?" added Joe.

"I think so," Penny answered. "We've held the games and tournament for several years now while the maze was being restored. We know the routine pretty well." She looked out the window.

"Mom, it's going to be okay," Kay said. "I don't know where Dad is, but I'm sure he's all right. And Frank and Joe will find him. They're real pros, Mom—we can trust them to do the job."

"That's our cue," Frank said, standing up. "Okay, we're out of here. We'll keep in touch by phone. Be sure and call us if you hear anything."

The Hardys left the house and went to the vehicle court. "Ray said to take what we need," Joe said. "That one," he announced, pointing to an SUV.

Joe drove while Frank phoned Officer Chester and then the film studio. "Officer Chester is just leaving to come to EagleSpy," Frank reported when he'd finished with the calls. "He said he'd hook up with us there later. Skip Jennin is on call at the studio and said he'd be happy to set us up."

They made pretty good time getting to the village, and were happy to see that traffic was bumper-to-bumper in the other lane, headed back to EagleSpy.

The studio was housed in the buildings once used by the old marble mine. Skip took them into a small screening room. All the film so far from all the cameras had been spliced into one long video.

Skip set up the film on a full-size movie screen to make it easier to watch. Then he showed the boys how to fast-forward, slow-forward, reverse, and pause, and how to zoom in on a certain part of an object. He also showed them how to determine where they were at any given moment in the footage, so they could make a note and he could pull up that image whenever they wanted. Then he left them and went back to his own work.

There were hundreds of yards of film, and the Hardys were determined to check out every inch that was shot on Friday afternoon and evening. Having four eyes helped.

Frank watched for Blackstone and followed the fire-eater when he was on-screen. Joe concentrated solely on finding the man he had seen running into the woods. Neither boy spoke for the first half hour. Then Frank broke the silence. "Wait a minute," he said. "Stop the film."

Joe hit the pause button on the console in front of his chair.

"Look," Frank said. "There's the fire-eater behind the stands. Who's he talking to?" The fire-eater was head-to-head with someone whose back was to the camera. Joe zoomed in and hit the slow-forward button.

The fire-eater was listening intently and nodding as the other man talked. Then the other man turned his head slightly to the left, and Joe paused on the man's profile.

"Are you thinking what I'm thinking?" Frank asked.

"It could be. It *definitely* could be—"

"Vincenzo Blackstone!"

Frank made a quick note of the location of that shot on the video. The next image was taken at a totally different location, so Joe played the film again at regular speed.

They were able to fast-forward through some of it—close-ups of spectators, children playing, Alan giving speeches. They kept their eyes open, but neither saw any glimpses of their three targets: Blackstone, Fire-Eater, or Running Guy.

Then finally, after an hour and twenty minutes, Joe spotted his man. "There! That's him! That's the guy I saw. I'm sure of it." He zoomed in on a large, stocky man in a silver-colored armor chestplate and belted peplum, chain mail sleeves and leggings, and knee-high cuffed black boots.

"No bow," Frank pointed out. "No arrows. And that helmet completely shields his face." The man walked around the back of the empty stands. The timer said it was 6:22 Friday evening.

"Everyone else was at the maze at that time," Joe said. "And the arrow hadn't been shot yet."

The man hurried to the end of the stands, and then turned in toward the stadium and disappeared.

The next shots were of the burning hedge. Joe switched to slow-forward and scanned every part of the screen as the images crept along. "Hold it," he said. "Look at that." He zoomed in on the edge of the picture. Barely visible in the surrounding darkness, a man walked forward from behind the maze.

"It's the fire-eater," Frank said, almost whispering. "That must have been when he joined in to help put out the fire."

"Right. But what was he doing behind the maze before that? No one was supposed to be back there."

Frank made another note about the location of that shot on the film. They watched until the end of Friday's shoot, went back to view a few places a second time, and then turned off the machine.

"There's still all of yesterday's film to see," Joe said, without much enthusiasm.

"I know, and we might want to check it out eventually," Frank said. "But if that was Blackstone talking to the fire-eater, and if the fire-eater was off-limits behind the maze . . ."

"You're right. We need to find that guy."

"Your woods-runner was so disguised that we can't really tell who he might be. And if he's out of disguise, we still won't recognize him."

"Right again," Joe said. "I have an idea, though." He led Frank out of the screening room and found Skip. Then he gave the filmmaker the location numbers for the images they wanted.

Skip printed still shots of the fire-eater walking from behind the maze and talking to the man behind the stadium stands. Then he blew up the shot of the other man's profile and compared it to the mug shot Frank showed him of Blackstone.

Skip scanned the mug shot into a computer and pulled up the two heads together on a monitor screen. "This design software is great," he explained. "I can take your photo and the software will age it so you'll know how you'll look thirty years from now. Or I can change your face any way you want—different nose, different eye color."

He clicked the computer mouse a couple of times. "Or I can do this," he said. He turned the straight-on face of Blackstone to a profile shot. Then he pulled the profile image of the man behind the stands around to a facing shot. All four heads belonged to the same man: Vincenzo Blackstone.

He printed several copies of the images for the Hardys, and they thanked him and left.

"This is real evidence," Joe said as he revved up the SUV.

"Computer-adjusted photos don't hold up in all courts yet," Frank said. "But they sure help police home in on a suspect. It looks like Blackstone not only is in the vicinity, but seems to be working with the fire-eater."

"That's how he operates," Joe reminded his brother. "He hires other people to do his dirty work."

"I want to talk to that talent agency in Halifax and find out more about the fire-eater," Frank said, dialing his cell phone, "but it's Sunday. I'll bet they're not open." He listened for a few minutes, then left his name and number on the agency's voice mail, adding that it was urgent that they call back. "Officer Chester might be able to track down the agency owner today, though," he said, closing his phone. "And the fire-eater might even be working at EagleSpy again this evening."

"Let's split up as soon as we get there," Joe suggested. "We should each take a packet of the mug shots and the profile shots."

"You find Officer Chester first—tell him what we know, show him what we've got. Don't forget to give him the message that Blackstone sent you. I'll find a Horton and see if the fire-eater is working today. If he is, I'll go after him right away."

Joe drove back to EagleSpy in record time. As they pulled in, one of the gatekeepers stopped them. "Hey, you're Joe Hardy, right?" he asked.

"I am," Joe answered.

"I've got a message for you," the young man said, and handed Joe a note.

Joe thanked him and read the brief message. "It's from Shorty. He says he found something that might help identify the man who ran into the woods Friday night. Shorty's working all day, but wants to meet me at his flat at about seven."

"Sounds good," Frank said. "You've got about an hour and a half to find Officer Chester."

Joe let Frank out near the stadium and continued on to return the car to the vehicle court.

Frank hurried inside the stadium and found Kay. "Is the fire-eater working today?" he asked.

"Yes, later this afternoon. But I thought I saw him in the bazaar a little while ago. Why?"

"I just want to talk to him. See you later," Frank said, hurrying off.

"Wait a minute," Kay called after him. "I'm coming with you."

Frank and Kay wove in and out of the crowd that shuffled along in the bazaar. Occasionally, Frank would stop at a booth and ask a vendor about the fire-eater. A few recognized the photos and said they'd seen him earlier. One person had seen Blackstone and the fire-eater pass by ten minutes earlier.

"Blackstone!" Kay yelled.

"Keep your voice down," Frank warned her. "We don't want them to know we're following them."

"But they have to be just ahead. Come on! We'll lose them." She zigzagged through the shoppers before Frank could stop her.

"Kay, wait!" Frank yelled, racing after her. "Stop!"

"I see his ponytail," Kay called back. "The fire-eater's. He just went around that booth. Hurry, Frank," she said as she disappeared from Frank's sight.

Her scream felt like a lance, stabbing into Frank's gut. Other yells and screams joined Kay's, and Frank flew through the crowd so fast, it felt as if his feet hardly touched ground.

He smelled the fire before he saw it. It had an oily smell that seemed to coat the inside of his nose and slither down his throat. Frank finally reached the small crowd gathering around the billowing smoke. He pushed his way through to find the source of the smoke: a ring of fire broiling up from the ground. In the center stood Kay, her eyes wide with the reflections of flames.

10 Fly-by-Knight

"Frank!" Kay called from inside the ring of fire. "Get me out of here!" The diameter of the circle was only about five or six feet, so Frank knew he had to act fast.

"Stand still, Kay," Frank yelled. His throat immediately filled with oily black smoke. "Cover your face," he told her. Kay put her hands up to protect her face.

Frank peeled off his jacket and slammed it down onto the flames. But the moving air just seemed to breathe more life into the fire. Some people in the crowd had drinks that they threw on the flames, but it wasn't enough to calm the fire.

Frank looked around. The stadium was about thirty yards away, and he remembered the big barrels of sand and sawdust sitting around the outside. Ray had told him they used them to replenish the stadium floor during the jousting matches.

"Come on!" he ordered, motioning to a strong-looking young man. The two boys raced to the stadium and grabbed one of the barrels. It had no lid, so they wouldn't be able to roll it back without spilling all the contents. But they could rock and roll it around on its bottom rim without losing too much. Frank's helper was as strong as he looked, and between them they maneuvered the heavy barrel back in just a few minutes.

Pushing the crowd back even farther, they lowered the barrel and began rolling it around the ring of fire. The sand and sawdust cascaded out over the flames and snuffed them instantly.

Kay jumped out of danger as Frank and the other man continued around the circle, extinguishing the whole fire. A couple of security guards arrived with fire extinguishers and made sure the job was complete.

Frank ran back to Kay. "What happened?" he asked.

"It was all so fast," Kay said. "I was following the fire-eater, and then I saw Vincenzo Blackstone, too. He turned quickly and recognized me. When he ducked around the booth, I followed. And the fire-eater was waiting for me with this can of—something. He sprayed it around the ground with one hand and set fire to it with the other. The ground just burst into flames in seconds. I didn't have a chance to get out before I was completely trapped in this awful circle."

"He just happened to have this fire-making stuff?" Frank asked.

"He had a bag over his shoulder. I've seen him off by himself before, rehearsing his act. He probably had some of that stuff in the bag in case he wanted to practice."

"Only this time, he decided to practice on you," Frank said, shaking his head. "Are you sure you're all right?"

"Sure, just a little shaky. But I'm okay." She took a glass of water someone offered her and sipped it slowly.

"What happened to Blackstone? Did you see which way he went?" Frank asked.

"Yes. They both headed for the woods over there," she answered, pointing.

"What happened?" Officer Chester asked, hurrying over to Frank. "I was talking to your brother by the stadium when I heard all the commotion over here. We could see the fire but figured it was the entertainer putting on a show. Someone just told me it wasn't an act."

"The fire-eater and Blackstone went into the woods over there," Frank said, turning on his heels. He sped across the meadow to the edge of the small forest, and heard Officer Chester and others pounding along behind him.

When they got to the edge of the woods, they were greeted by the fire-eater, his hands high in the air. "Don't shoot or anything," he yelled. "Please. I'll tell you anything you want. I never meant to hurt anyone."

"Well, you came way too close," Frank said through gritted teeth. He could feel all kinds of alien things in his mouth—oily residue from the fire, grit, and sawdust. He spat out some of the gunk and turned back to the fire-eater. "Where's Vincenzo Blackstone?" he demanded.

"Already on the road, probably," the fire-eater said, his hands still up in the air. "I'm supposed to be helpin' him. I'm supposed to be his partner! Some partner. When the law starts closin' in, he ditches me and saves his own sweet skin. He had a car hidden here in the woods. It's already gone. But I can tell you where he might be goin'. He's been stayin' with my friends in a fishin' shack the other side of the village. I'll be happy to help you find him."

"Where's Alan Horton?" Frank asked.

"Hey, I don't know," the fire-eater said. "Probably in the stadium, or workin' on the maze. That's what I was hired for—to keep the maze from openin'. That's all I know about."

"Did you shoot the flaming arrow, or did Blackstone?" Officer Chester asked.

"I'm telling you, my only job was bringing down the maze. That Blackstone's some kind of computer whiz, so he tripped the security system and in we went. I was in there Friday night with Blackstone, and we messed it up pretty good. I only heard about the arrow when we came back out."

"You mean Blackstone was with you in the maze when the arrow was shot?" Frank said.

"He was," the fire-eater said.

"Well, I don't believe that for a minute," Officer Chester said, handcuffing his prisoner. "Come on—we're going to find your partner."

"I'm going back to help Kay," Frank told the officer. "Let me know what happens with Blackstone."

"We'll keep in touch," Officer Chester said, walking his prisoner back to the police car.

Frank found Kay with her mother and Ray in the stadium and told them all about the arrest. It was nearly seven o'clock.

Across the field, Joe checked his watch. It was 6:50. He looked around for Frank but didn't see him, so he headed for the stables. The sun had already set behind the trees, and the automatic lights had clicked on outside the building.

Joe strolled along the stalls, clicking his tongue at the horses, but no humans were around. He walked up the steps to Shorty's apartment, knocked on the door, and called out the trainer's name. There was no response.

Back down in the stables, he found the two horses belonging to the Donaldsons and scrunched down onto a hay bale outside their stalls to wait.

After a while he checked his watch again. Twenty minutes had passed, and Shorty had not shown up. "So he's working with animals," Joe muttered to himself. "And they're not always on schedule."

Fifteen more minutes passed, and it was getting a lot darker inside the stables. Only the three outside lights were on, casting eerie shapes of light inside and across the floor. Joe walked over to the large light switch by the open door and yanked the handle up, but nothing happened. There was a click, but no light.

Immediately, Joe felt that familiar spiky tickling across the back of his neck. His instincts told him something was awry. As if reading his mind, a few horses began moving around in their stalls, twitching their tails and bobbing their heads.

Joe's senses instantly rose into high alert, but he knew better than to just jump and run. *If this is a trap,* he asked himself, *where's the danger? Am I safer in here?* He strained his eyes so he could see through the dark shadows inside the stables. *Or should I make a run for it?*

Keeping his back against the wall so his body

faced into the stables, he turned his head to look outside the open door next to him. Although there were patches of ground bathed in large swaths of light, there was even more darkness—plenty of places to conceal an ambush.

Some of the horses seemed to grow more nervous—pawing the ground and sending small snorts out into the stable silence.

Joe felt a new urgency, and he knew it was time to make a move. It was ten to eight already, so he decided to make one more try at Shorty's apartment. "Maybe he went up from an outside door," Joe whispered to the horses as he hurried past their stalls. "Maybe he was up there when I knocked earlier, but he was asleep and didn't hear me. Or maybe—"

Joe didn't finish his thought. He didn't want to guess what else could have happened to Shorty.

He was more cautious this time as he climbed the flight of wooden steps next to the last stall. He reached the small landing and put his ear to Shorty's door, but he heard nothing.

He decided not to knock this time, and cautiously tried the doorknob. It turned easily. He waited until the shiver had finished rippling down his back. Then he slowly inched the door open. A thin bolt of moonlight cut across the room.

There was hardly any sound at first, just a low

100

swoooooosh. Then he heard a sudden hollow-sounding clattering. He looked up just in time to see the falcon's talons glint in the moonlight as they shot toward his face.

11 The Phantom Archer

By the time he saw the falcon zooming toward him,
it was too late to close the door. Joe dove facedown
on the floor, covering his head with his arms. He
heard a *thunk* from above and realized the falcon
must have banged into the doorsill. He felt a thud
on the back of his leg and then a pain so intense that
he temporarily lost his voice and couldn't even yell.

He whipped around in time to see the falcon
shoot through the door and down into the stables.
He couldn't see his leg very clearly in the darkness.
But he felt the rip in his jeans and the sticky wet-
ness oozing from his calf.

He rolled up to stand, and felt a new wave of
pain. Limping and hopping, he went down the
steps and out of the stables. He had gone only a

few yards when Shorty pulled up in his golf cart.

"Hey, what happened to you?" he yelled to Joe, who hopped over to the cart.

"I was slashed by a peregrine," Joe said, hoisting his leg into the passenger seat. "In your flat."

"What?! What do you mean, my flat? How did you . . . why were you . . . no, never mind, we'll talk about that later," he added, spotting the blood soaking through Joe's jeans. "We have to get you to the hospital!"

Shorty helped Joe over to his car, where Joe lay down in the backseat. They then sped into the village.

"Don't be concerned about how small our little hospital is," Shorty assured him. "It might not be the place you'd want for a kidney transplant, but for a falcon slashing, it's perfect."

"Glad to hear that," Joe said. He was feeling a little woozy, although his leg had finally managed to stop his bleeding all over Shorty's car.

"So what were you doing at my place?" Shorty asked.

"What do you mean?" Joe said. "You told me to meet you there."

"And exactly when was it that I said that?"

"In the note the gatekeeper gave me," Joe said. He fished into his jeans pocket and pulled out the folded paper. Then he lobbed it over into the front passenger seat.

Shorty reached over and unfolded the paper. He scanned the note quickly and then got his eyes back on to the road. "Interesting," he said. "I didn't write that note. I never set up that meeting with you."

"'Set up' seems to be the right term," Joe said, shaking his head. "It was a total trap. Were you scheduled for something specific at seven?"

"Sure," he answered. "That was the jousting semi-pros. I handle all the horses for all the matches. The games were scheduled for six to ten, and I'm booked solid the whole time."

"So anyone who knows the schedule and knows that you handle the horses would know that you wouldn't be in your flat during that time."

"That's right," Shorty said.

"What do you know about the falconer who entertained the crowd on Friday night?" Joe asked.

"He's a good man," Shorty said, "a personal friend. He's employed by Mr. Horton, and lives not far from here."

"Does anyone else keep falcons in this area?"

Shorty chuckled. "Yes, sir. We've got several. Believe it or not, a couple are still using them for hunting ducks, pheasants, and such."

"So it wouldn't be too hard to find one or buy one or *steal* one around here," Joe concluded.

"Not if you knew what to look for," Shorty agreed. "'Course, you'd have to know a little bit about handling one too. If you want, I'll ask around the falconers I know. See if anyone's been selling lately or had one go missing."

"That'd be great, Shorty," Joe said. "Thanks." Joe felt himself drifting off into a drowsy state—not quite sleep and not quite unconscious.

Shorty's voice pulled him back. "Here we are," he said. "Just lie still. I'll get the medics."

Within just a couple of minutes, Shorty returned with two doctors and a gurney. They lifted Joe gingerly onto the mattress and wheeled him into an examining room. Another doctor and two nurses were waiting for him.

The emergency team worked quickly, cutting off Joe's jeans leg, cleaning and dressing the wound, taking a blood sample to check for infection and clotting factor, and giving him an IV boost of fluids and antibiotics to help jump-start his healing process.

Then the doctor slowly, systematically stitched up the eight-inch slash.

"You were very lucky," the doctor told him after he'd finished and they'd moved Joe to a bed. "Those talons are like razors, but they missed the tendons, ligaments, and major vessels in your calf. You're going to be really sore for a while and hobbling around with a crutch or cane. But the wound should heal up nicely."

"But I can leave now, right?" Joe asked. "I don't have to stay here overnight or anything?"

"No, you can go. I'll give you some literature to

read so you can watch for signs of infection. And I'll need to see you again tomorrow and the next day to change the dressing." He handed Joe some pamphlets and flyers about wild bird attacks.

"You're not local," the doctor said. "Where are you staying?"

"At EagleSpy."

"Ah, you're part of the festivities going on out there, are you?"

"Yes, sort of. My brother and I are actually guests of the Hortons. We're old friends of Ray's."

"Well, then, you're really in luck. Penny Horton is a registered nurse. If she consents, I will allow her to change your dressing and monitor your vital signs. You won't have to come back here unless there's a problem."

"Perfect," Joe said. He attempted to sit in the bed, but he felt woozy and fell back on the pillow.

"We've given you some medication that will knock you out for a little while," the nurse told him. "Your body needs rest after such a shock. You lost a lot of blood. We'll lend you a crutch and a cane until you either get your own or no longer need them."

The nurse soon pushed Joe in a wheelchair out of the small emergency room. The pamphlets, flyers, crutch, and cane were draped awkwardly over his lap. He was glad to finally lie down on the backseat of Shorty's car again, and he fell asleep almost immediately.

Shorty had called ahead to Penny, and she and Frank were waiting for Joe when he arrived. Shorty and Frank helped Joe into a guest room on the first floor that Penny had fixed up for him.

"No point in making you climb the stairs," she said. "And you have your own bathroom right here." She opened the door next to the closet.

Penny looked over at Frank. "I can never thank you enough for rescuing Kay this evening," she said. "If it hadn't been for you, I might be fixing this room up for *her* recovery."

"That's okay, Penny," Frank said. "I'm happy everything worked out."

Shorty and Penny left while Frank helped Joe strip down to sleep shorts and shirt and pile into the comfortable bed.

"Looks like you'll need a new partner in the maze relay," Joe said with a crooked smile. "What's this about rescuing Kay?"

"I'll tell you about that in a minute," Frank said. "First, tell me what happened to you."

Joe described his wait for Shorty at the stables and the subsequent peregrine attack. "I was set up," he concluded. "Shorty's going to check around and see who might have planted the falcon there. Probably Blackstone or one of his thugs."

"Blackstone's in jail," Frank announced with a big grin. He told Joe about tailing the fire-eater and Blackstone through the bazaar and rescuing Kay from the ring of fire.

"Officer Chester called Penny a half hour ago," Frank reported. "They caught Blackstone. He's cooling off in the village jail. The fire-eater has agreed to spill everything. Both of them insist they had nothing to do with the arrow or Alan's disappearance. But the police don't believe that story. Officer Chester is having the arrow shaft traced. If he can prove a connection between it and Blackstone . . ."

"What do you think?" Joe asked his brother.

"I don't know. The fire-eater seems willing to confess about the maze destruction and the vicious assault on Kay—although he swears he never meant that fire to get so out of hand."

"So you think he'd confess to the flaming arrow and to kidnapping Alan if he'd done those, too?" Joe said. "Kidnapping's pretty serious—it might be more than he's willing to admit."

"True, but he came pretty close to attempted murder or manslaughter with that fire. And he seems to be willing to do anything to keep himself out of prison. I just think that if he knew where Alan is, he'd tell the cops."

"Even if the fire-eater didn't have anything to do with the rest of it, that doesn't mean that Blackstone's hands are clean. Maybe Vincenzo pulled off the kidnapping by himself—or hired someone else to do it."

"I can't shake the feeling that there's something more going on," Frank said. "Maybe when Shorty checks out the falconers, we'll get a new lead that I can go after tomorrow. I also want to check out the caretaker's cottage."

"Ray and I didn't notice anything—except the smell of cooked fish."

"I know, but you didn't have time to give it a real search. I've searched for Alan in every building on EagleSpy except that one. I need to tie up that loose end."

"I hear you," Joe said, "and you're right."

"Meanwhile, you get some sleep and get well," Frank said. He propped up Joe's leg with a pillow, turned out the light, and went upstairs to his own bed.

Joe sat up suddenly. It was pitch black and the only sound he heard was the large grandfather clock. *Bong . . . bong . . . bong.*

"Where am I?" he muttered, fumbling at the side of the bed for a light. He swung his legs around and sat on the edge of the bed. He felt dizzy for a few seconds, but then got his bearings.

His left leg felt thick and clumsy . . . weird.

He moved his hands around until he finally

found a lamp, fumbled for the switch, and turned it on. It was only a sixty-watt bulb, so it illuminated just a small area.

This isn't my room, he thought, looking over to where Frank's bed should be. There was a small chest there instead. Then he noticed the bottle of antibiotics on the table next to the bed. All of Sunday's memories tumbled through his brain like a tidal wave. The message in his computer . . . the film footage . . . Blackstone and the fire-eater . . . the stables . . . the falcon.

He reached down and gingerly touched his thick padded wound dressing. His leg was a little sore, but it wasn't too bad. If the grandfather clock was right and it was three o'clock, he figured he'd been asleep for about four hours. And now he was wide awake.

He was also hungry. He couldn't remember eating anything since the sandwiches and soup they'd had in the kitchen. And that had been more than twelve hours ago.

He slid off the bed onto his good leg. Then he cautiously lowered his slashed leg and carefully transferred his weight onto it a little at a time. He felt a little pang when he stepped on it, but it wasn't anything he couldn't tolerate.

A stack of his clothes sat on the chair by the bathroom. Joe cleaned up a little, pulled on a pair of jeans, a T-shirt, and his cross-trainers, and limped into the kitchen. He didn't hear a sound from the bedrooms upstairs.

He headed straight for the refrigerator. "Mmmmm . . . turkey, roast beef, cheese, pickles," he murmured, stacking it all on a tray. "I can fix one gigantic sandwich." He added a piece of pie, a quart of milk, and a bottle of water. Then he took his food over to the long table and, perched on a stool, dug into his meal.

While he ate, he looked out the wide window that captured the vista of gardens and meadow between the house and the maze. A full moon in a cloudless sky lit the landscape like a spotlight. In the distance, the outside hedge wall of the maze seemed capped in silvery moonshine.

"Is that really moonlight?" he wondered aloud. He limped over to the window and picked up the binoculars sitting on the sill. An eerie glow hung over the maze. "I remember that glow," Joe whispered to no one. "We saw it when Alan turned on the night-lights last Friday. But this time, the lights aren't on, are they? Of course there was no moon on Friday, and there's a big one tonight. But . . ."

There's only one way to find out, he thought. He wasn't going to be in the maze races, anyway. There was no reason why he couldn't check it out.

He put the food back in the refrigerator, and got a flashlight, pen, and notebook from a drawer in the long table. Then he grabbed a barn jacket from the hook on the kitchen door and limped out to the vehicle court. All the golf carts still had the keys in their ignitions, so he started one up and headed for the maze.

As he grew nearer, he saw that the glow above the hedges was different from how it had been with the night-lights on. And when he finally began limping through the maze, he saw that the electric lights were not on. *It's the moonlight,* he thought. *It makes it seem like a whole other world in here.*

The flashlight stayed in his hip pocket as he followed the hedge tunnels through the maze. He drew a sort of diagram of his trail in the notebook as he limped along, so he'd be sure to find his way back out.

The maze was very elaborate, with lots of side paths, dead ends, and loop-backs. After backtracking out of several dead ends, he finally reached the repaired center of the maze. The only signs of the reconstruction were the new hedges. They were paler and not as full and lush as the others.

The maze center was laid out like a small oval park, with carved wooden benches and clumps of flowers. The ground was littered with smooth black pebbles that crunched as he walked. A mailbox was near one of the benches.

Joe remembered Ray telling him that clues for the maze scavenger hunt would be left in the mailboxes scattered along the paths. He opened the box and took out a piece of paper with lines printed on it in some sort of pattern. It looked vaguely familiar, but he was feeling very tired and the medicine had dulled his brain.

He was also becoming acutely aware of his aching leg wound. He shoved the paper in his pocket, plopped onto one of the benches, and stretched his leg out on the seat. He even leaned his head back on the top of the bench and closed his eyes for a few minutes.

The first rustling seemed far away, as if it was coming from the far outside wall of the maze. But when he heard it again, it seemed a little closer, then closer still. It wasn't a loud noise, but more like someone blowing on the hedge leaves or turning the pages of a book.

Opening his eyes, Joe looked toward the direction of the slight sound. The glow above the hedges was brighter there and seemed to be moving toward him along with the rustling sound.

He watched and listened for a few seconds, then realized he was holding his breath. He let it out at once with a sigh. At that same moment, the rustling noise seemed to move across a path next to his bench, and the leaves in one tall hedge fluttered.

Joe squinted and strained to see what was moving in the moonshine. And then, like a burst of greenish silver light, the ghostly specter of a man materialized from the hedge wall and floated over the pebbles.

12 Cracking the Code

The ghostly image never looked Joe's way. He was dressed all in white: white shirt, white slacks, and white shoes. Balding at the front of his scalp, he sported a shock of pale hair that started halfway back and streaked out behind his head. He had deep-set eyes and a neatly trimmed mustache and beard. In his left hand he carried a cluster of sleek arrows. His right hand held a long white bow.

Joe gasped as the specter slowly sailed over the path and was swallowed by the opposite hedge wall. His feet never crunched the pebbles.

The glowing aura above the hedge seemed to recede, and it grew darker. Joe's aching leg began to tremble, and he slowly lowered it to the ground. He stared at the path where he had seen the ghostly archer. Then he limped over to the exact places where the ghost had first materialized and then disappeared. The hedges were completely whole, no broken branches or fallen leaves. There was no sign that anyone—or anything—had passed through them.

He hopped and limped around the end of the hedge wall and stared into the next row. He thought he saw a white leg curl around the corner, so he hustled as fast as he could to the end of *that* row and turned into the next path. It was one of the maze's one hundred dead ends, and there was no man in white to be seen.

Joe shook his head. "It's the medicine," he muttered. "It *has* to be." He checked the diagram of the path he'd taken through the maze, but he could no longer read it clearly. Clouds had formed in the previously starry sky, masking the moon and forcing Joe to use his flashlight to see his way out.

At last he reached the entrance again. He let out another sigh and climbed painfully into the golf cart. By the time he was finally back in his new bed, he had decided that the archer in the maze had been a hallucination. As he fell asleep, he wasn't even sure he'd been to the maze at all.

Monday morning, Frank woke early and cleaned up fast. He knew he had a lot to do—more than usual, since his brother was temporarily laid up. He took the stairs two at a time and went into the downstairs bedroom that Penny had fixed up for Joe.

"Hey great, you're awake," Frank said. Joe was dressed and sitting on a chair.

"Hey yourself," Joe said.

"How are you feeling?"

"My leg's a lot better, but my mind's still kind of fuzzy. These antibiotics are better than going to the movies. I dreamed I woke up and was hungry, so I fixed a sandwich. Then I took a golf cart out to the maze, limped around inside, and saw this guy floating around through the hedges like a ghost."

Joe pulled on his shoes, and a smooth black pebble dropped onto the carpet.

"What's that?" Frank asked.

"It's a pebble," Joe said, looking amazed, "like the ones I saw in my dream in the center of the maze. There are benches and these pebbles all over the ground."

"Are you saying it might have been real? You actually went to the maze?"

"Maybe," Joe said quietly, leading Frank out the door and into the kitchen. Joe was relieved to see that he was moving a lot better. His leg ached and was tender if he stepped on it a certain way, but it was more flexible than it had been the day before, and he felt stronger.

"We're having breakfast out here," Penny called to the Hardys from the sunroom.

Frank and Joe started down the small corridor toward the sunroom, but only Frank made it. He turned back to see where his brother was. Joe was staring at a small oil painting hanging in a corner beside the butler's pantry. In it, a tall man stood drawing back a bowstring and arrow in perfect archer's form. He was dressed in a uniform of white shoes, white slacks, and white long-sleeved shirt with a banded collar.

"He's pretty impressive," Frank said, walking over to examine the painting.

"This is the guy in my dream," Joe said. His voice was low, almost a whisper.

"You're kidding."

"I'm *not* kidding. Don't say anything to the others about it yet." Joe walked slowly into the sunroom, and he and Frank joined the others around a table in the corner.

"Wow. Joe, you're walking so much better," Kay said. "Amazing what a good night's sleep can do."

"It sure is," Joe said, helping himself to eggs and sausage. "I just noticed the painting in the hallway—the archer. Does he live around here?"

"You might say that," Ray answered with a chuckle. "He's in a grave on the far end of the estate."

"Excuse me?" Joe said. He hoped the Hortons didn't notice the goose bumps on his arms.

"It's the baron," Penny said. "Baron Jackson Brighthall, the original owner of this property, the last in the long line of Brighthalls who lived here. He's been dead for years. He was a champion Olympic archer in the last century—we think that's what the painting is supposed to represent."

"Did you know him?" Joe asked.

"No. He met his untimely death a decade before Dad bought the property," Kay said.

"What do you mean 'untimely'?" Frank asked, pouring himself a cup of coffee.

"He was murdered," Kay said, crouching over her plate. "And the murder has never been solved to this day. No one lived here in the years before we bought it, and the place just decayed. But the baron's presence was still very much around."

"How do you mean?" Joe asked, although he was sure he knew what she was going to say next.

"Villagers would troop across the grounds to get to the beach or to go fishing from the jetty," Kay continued. "Many of them reported seeing the baron's ghost slipping around the crumbling walls and decaying topiary trees."

Frank and Joe exchanged glances, but stuck to their mutual agreement to not tell the Hortons yet about Joe's maze adventure.

"So what's on the schedule today?" Frank asked the Hortons.

"More of the same," Penny said matter-of-factly. "More competitions, a couple of races, the bazaar. If Vincenzo kidnapped Alan, I'm hoping he or the fire-eater will tell the police where he is today, so we can bring him home."

"You said 'if' Vincenzo kidnapped him," Joe repeated. "Do you have another theory?"

"No . . . no, not really," Penny said, with a forced smile. "And what about you two? What's next in the investigation?"

The Hardys told the others about checking over the film footage and what they had seen. "Blackstone and the fire-eater insist they had nothing to do with the flaming arrow," Frank reported. "It could be true. If they were trashing the center of the maze, there's no way they could be shooting the arrow from the other side too."

"So you're back to the man running into the woods?" Ray said.

"He's all we've got at this point," Joe told them. "Everyone else in the crowd was gathered at the maze entrance. He was the only one seen first hanging around the stands and then running away."

"But Blackstone hired the fire-eater," Kay said. "Couldn't he have hired the flaming arrow archer, too?"

"That's what we thought at first," Frank said. "But he told Officer Chester that he was thrilled to hear about the flaming arrow because he figured that guy would also be blamed for trashing the maze, and all suspicion would be diverted from Blackstone's team."

"He usually loves to take credit for ruining someone else's creation," Penny said.

"Yes, but he's been in a lot of trouble lately—and is about to be charged here," Joe pointed out. "So maybe he can't afford to take on any more—especially if it's someone else's crime."

"Like I said, we're back to the guy running away," Ray said.

"Has anyone seen Bruce MacLaren around since Alan threw him out of the stadium and off the property?" Joe asked. "The running guy was built a lot like MacLaren, although since he was in a costume, I can't be sure. The *B* on the arrow could fit, though."

"No one's reported a sighting of him to us," Penny said. "Alan alerted all the security people to watch for him and not allow him on the property again."

"Well, I'm off to talk to Shorty about Joe's falcon incident," Frank said. "Maybe we can get a lead there."

"Joe, you're staying in and resting, I hope," Penny said. "The doctor has placed you in my charge. You'd better be a good patient!"

"I'm going to stay down for a while, at least," Joe said. "You three go on out and run the show. But let's all keep in touch by phone."

"Don't forget the baron," Kay called after them as the Hardys left the sunroom. "He was an ace archer. Maybe his ghost shot the flaming arrow!"

Back in Joe's room, the Hardys closed the door for a private strategy session. "So the baron's ghost was hanging around the maze last night," Frank said, shaking his head. "I'm not going to accept that explanation until we cancel out the other possibilities."

"Like someone pretending to be a ghost to try and scare people off," Joe offered.

"Exactly," Frank said. "And when we find out who, we'll find out why."

"Or vice versa."

They decided that Frank would check in with Shorty about the falcon and with the falconer himself if necessary. Then he was going to search the caretaker's cottage. Joe would call Officer Chester and get an update on Blackstone.

"Would you bring me my computer before you leave?" Joe asked. "I want to dig up some more stuff on Bruce MacLaren."

Frank brought the computer down for Joe. "Did I tell you Blackstone admitted to hacking into your computer and leaving that message?" Frank asked.

"Guess we showed him who the amateur is, didn't we?" Joe said with a broad grin. Frank returned the smile and left for the stables.

Joe called the police station immediately. Officer Chester was still there. He reported that Blackstone and the fire-eater were sticking to their stories about what they did and didn't do. He also said the arrow Frank had found was a true antique, but they'd had no luck tracing it to Blackstone.

Joe fired up his computer and spent the next several hours gathering data. He was still clicking away when Frank slammed into the room. "Look!" he said, waving some brochures at Joe. "Look what I found at one of the bazaar booths."

Joe thumbed through the brochures while Frank kept talking. "They're codes," he said. "Some of them ancient, some more modern. This vendor had all sorts of books and samples of codes that have been used through the ages—the Rosetta stone, runes, secret alphabets, international spy codes."

"Hey, this looks like—"

"Exactly," Frank said, pulling a page out of his pocket. "Remember this? I found it in Alan's secret study. We thought it might be a maze design, but it's a code." Frank pulled out one of the brochures. "See? It's like this one. Each of these lines or collection of lines represents a letter of the alphabet. Once you decrypt the code, you can read the message."

"Wait a minute," Joe said, reaching into his jeans pocket. "I forgot all about this. I thought it looked familiar, but I was too foggy last night to put it all together." He showed Frank the note he had found in the maze mailbox.

"It's the same code," Frank said. "Wow, maybe it *does* have something to do with the maze puzzle and the competition."

"What else were you thinking?"

"I don't know. I thought it might mean something bigger." He looked at the two pieces of paper and seemed lost in thought.

"What did Shorty say about the falcon?" Joe asked, pulling Frank's attention back.

"It was not one of the Hortons' falconer's birds. It belonged to a local farmer. It's been missing for a couple of days—the guy didn't know what had happened to it."

"Stolen," Joe concluded. "My meeting was a setup, so there's no way that the falcon being in there was a coincidence."

"Right," Frank agreed. "Did you talk to Officer Chester?"

Joe told his brother what the policeman had reported. "But I've got bigger news than that," he continued. "Look at this." He punched in a few letters on his computer keyboard, then clicked the mouse. The screen filled with a familiar top security identification.

"You tapped into Dad's files."

"I did," Joe said. "It's okay—this qualifies."

The Hardys' father, Fenton, was a career law enforcement officer, and served as a consultant on many international cases for government and private organizations. His top security files were accessible only with a series of passwords. He had entrusted those to his sons with the instruction to use them only for extreme emergencies. They had always honored this responsibility.

"We entered these files once when Dad was kidnapped," Frank said. "The kidnapping of a friend's father also qualifies."

"Right," Joe said with a click. "I looked up Blackstone first, and found only the maze vandalism in Scotland. Then I found Bruce MacLaren. He's got a petty criminal record: gambling, a few assault arrests—nothing major. The twins were right about his family being a bunch of thieves, deserters, and gamblers. But Bruce also has another interesting talent. He, too, was an Olympic archer." The screen filled with data on MacLaren.

Frank thumbed through the brochures from the code vendor. Then he looked at the two pieces of paper they'd found that were scribbled in code. "Look up Alan," he said quietly.

"Alan? Why?"

"Just a hunch. Look him up."

Joe punched in a few letters and clicked the mouse. "Hmmmmm, that's weird," he murmured. He punched again and clicked. "Totally weird," he said.

"What's happening?"

"That's just it," Joe answered. "Nothing. The file is labeled 'Highest Security Only' and requires four more passwords."

"Whoa, that's new," Frank said, looking over Joe's shoulder.

"And check out Alan's code name for this file," Joe said, reading it aloud. "EagleSpy."

13 The Marble Shaft

"Alan Horton *is* EagleSpy," Frank repeated. "My hunch wasn't so far-fetched after all."

"Okay, now you *have* to tell me what you were talking about," Joe demanded.

"When I saw these code books, I was reminded of that piece of paper I found in Alan's secret study. It was definitely a code. Then I got to thinking about that room. It's like a safe room, a place where he might do secret work."

"And he got that weird phone call," Joe reminded them. "On a phone with no dialing mechanism—just two buttons. He said there were other entrances to that room too."

"Right. And didn't you say he seemed sort of freaked at first when the gauntlet wasn't there, but then said something about putting it somewhere else?"

"That's right. The story seemed kind of funny, but I just figured he didn't want me to know where it was."

"There's one more thing that seems odd. I think Penny's been kind of strange through this whole deal," Frank said. "It's almost as if she knows where Alan is. She doesn't seem to be really worried about him and what might have happened to him."

Joe looked back at his screen. "There's definitely some things we don't know about Alan Horton."

"Well, let's go see if we can find them out," Frank said. "Do you think you can handle the stairs?"

"Definitely," Joe said. "And I know just where we're going."

The Hardys went up the large staircase, then up the small one. Joe was a little slower than usual, but determined to follow Frank into Alan Horton's secret study.

The room looked exactly as it had shortly after they had learned that Alan had disappeared. "It doesn't look like anyone has been here since we came up before," Frank said, turning on the light and small fan hanging over the long drafting table.

"Let's find out if Alan was telling the truth about this room having other entrances," Joe said.

They began systematically checking every inch of the space—walls, ceiling, and floor. Joe started with the bookcase. He removed every book and flipped through the pages, looking for a key, a lock combination, a diagram of the room—anything that might indicate a hidden door or window. Then he tapped on the wall behind the books, listening for the hollow sound that might indicate something back there besides insulation.

Frank lifted the chair, slid the trunk, and rolled back the rug. There was nothing. Then he crawled under the long drafting table, pushing and pulling on the furniture, tapping the floor and wall. He removed all the drawers and felt all along the openings. There were no buttons to push, no levers to pull.

"Try the light," Joe called over his shoulder, as he pressed on every inch of every bookshelf.

Frank reached up to the light hanging over the worktable. He turned it off and on again, twisted it and turned it. Then he turned the fan off and back on. He looked up at the fixture in the ceiling. Then he pulled out his flashlight for a better look. "Well, what do you know," Frank said.

"What!" Joe said. "Is it something?"

"It's something. There are three switches on this fixture—one for the light, one for the fan, and one for . . ."

He hopped onto the table and stood up. His head grazed the ceiling as he pulled the third chain hanging from the fixture. A creaking noise filled

the little room immediately, then stopped. Then it started again, and the wall behind the little desk began to move to the right, like a pocket door. It slipped completely away, revealing a wide hallway beyond that ended in a door.

Frank jumped from the table and hurried down the hallway. Joe followed, his walking becoming more steady with each step.

Frank opened the door at the end of the hallway. "An elevator!" he said. "Let's go for it."

The Hardys got in the elevator and pushed the down button. It was a lurching, bumpy ride down to what seemed like five or six flights below. When it stopped, Joe opened the door. The distinctive smell immediately washed into the little room.

"We're in the mine," Frank said in a low voice. "We're in the marble mine. There's that weird metallic smell, and the gritty dust in the air. I'm sure that's where we are." He could see a long tunnel stretching out in front of the elevator.

"Probably not a good idea," Joe said, reading his brother's mind. "Moving this elevator through the ground might cause a cave-in."

"We need to get back up and check out the map," Frank said. "We can't be moving around down here without knowing where we are. It's too dangerous."

"Agreed," Joe said, closing the door. He pushed the second button, and the little room creaked upward. The trip seemed very slow. All he could think about was getting back aboveground and safely into the house. At last the elevator stopped, Joe opened the door, and they saw the welcome hallway back to Alan's secret study.

They arranged everything in the study the way they'd found it, closed the pocket door, turned out the light, and went back down to the first floor.

"Man, it's dark out," Joe said, hopping off the last step of the large curved staircase.

"A storm might be rolling in," Frank said, looking out the window. "But it's not raining yet. Kay and Penny are running up the drive now. Distract Kay for me, will you? I want to talk to Penny alone."

"Sure," Joe said.

Once Kay and Penny got to the house, Joe asked Kay out to the sunroom, saying he wanted to talk to her about MacLaren. Frank guided Penny into the library and closed the door.

"What's going on?" Penny asked.

"I just want to talk to you for a few minutes about EagleSpy," Frank said. "EagleSpy, the man—*not* the estate."

Penny stared at Frank for a few seconds without moving. Then she sighed and leaned back in her chair. "How long have you known?" she asked. "How did you figure it out?"

"That's not important right now," Frank said. "We have to find Alan. Tell me about his work—his work other than maze design."

"I will tell you because I respect you and your brother as detectives," Penny said, "and because Alan told me a couple of days ago that if something happened to him and you asked about his intelligence work, I was to tell you."

"He works in intelligence?" Frank asked. "As a cryptographer?"

"That's right," she said. "He creates codes and also decrypts codes for an international intelligence agency. Please understand that Kay and Ray do not know the entire story. They know that he has served in the military and has done some consulting for search-and-rescue organizations. They do not know the full extent of his work."

"We won't tell anyone what you tell us," Frank assured her. "Do you know where he is now? Has he contacted you since he's been gone?"

"No, he hasn't. When I first realized he was gone, I was frightened because of the maze incidents and that awful confrontation with Bruce MacLaren. But then I talked myself into thinking he might be on an assignment and just hasn't been able to contact me yet. Maybe I'm just fooling myself."

"That's what we're trying to find out," Frank said. "If he's on assignment or somewhere safe. We're going to be gone for a little while, but we'll probably want to talk to you some more when we get back."

"No problem," Penny said. "I'll do anything to help. I hope you know that."

They left the library, and Frank signaled to Joe to meet him in Joe's room. Joe arrived a few minutes later, and Frank told him what he'd learned from Penny. "I still want to check the caretaker's cottage," Frank said. "It's the only building on the estate that I haven't searched."

"I'm going too," Joe said. "I didn't have time for a real search either. But let's check the maps first. I want to see the ones for the mine, for the estate, and for the house. Maybe we can figure out where that elevator goes."

The Hardys spent an hour studying the maps that Kay gave them, trying to line up the mine with the house, and then the elevator with the mine. They finally decided that they had the mine location pinpointed, but they were unsure of how safe it might be in that area.

"It's the perfect place for a kidnapper to hide Alan, you know," Joe said. "He could take him away from the house without ever going outdoors."

"Which would explain why none of the vehicles were missing when he disappeared," Frank added.

The Hardys rolled up the maps and dropped them in a long plastic bag. Then they pulled on jackets, Frank grabbed his sports bag, and they left the house. A dirt road led directly to the cottage, so they took a small truck and drove off.

It still wasn't raining, but the sky had gotten even darker, and the wind was whipping around the truck cab. Frank drove, and Joe served as navigator. After about half an hour, Joe told Frank to start slowing down. "You'll have to park the truck up by those birch trees," he said, "and we'll walk the rest of the way."

They could see a narrow trail skirting the birch woods and leading toward the edge of the bluff where the cottage stood. From where they were, Golden Arm Lake looked dark and choppy.

Frank led the way. He was on guard and watchful as they quietly plodded along the trail. When they got to the cottage, it was just as Joe had described it. He peered through a partly broken window. The cottage looked empty and abandoned.

The first thing Joe noticed as they entered the cottage was an impressive collection of old archery equipment scattered in a corner. "Hmmmm, this looks familiar," he said. "Just like the set the baron carried as he flew by last night."

"Shhh, I heard something in the water," Frank whispered, motioning Joe to be quiet. But there were no sounds except the windblown waves of the lake tumbling onto the shore. Frank moved cautiously into the tiny bedroom at the back of the house.

"Must have been a fish jumping," Joe muttered. "By the way, I'm not picking up that greasy smell

today." He went to the little kitchen in the corner and began poking through pots and pans. Every once in a while he felt as if someone was watching him, and he turned his head around to check. But there was never anything to see but the walls of the dusty little cottage.

He didn't like having his back to the door, so he sped up his search, opening and closing cupboard doors and peering into drawers. There were a few plates and glasses, some forks, and a couple of knives. As Joe reached for the last cupboard door, his focus—and the silence—were shattered.

"Who are you?" rumbled a gravelly voice. "And what do you think you're doing?"

Joe turned slowly and faced the ghost of Baron Brighthall, standing in the dark cottage doorway.

14 An Unexpected Ally

"I asked you a question," the man yelled. "I thought I'd chased all you young people out of here. I told you to find another place for your beach parties. Now, get out!"

"Are you Baron Whitehall?" Joe said.

The man's expression changed instantly to shock, and then what looked like fear. He backed off the little step leading into the cottage, and Joe thought he was going to run.

"You're not going anywhere," Frank said, appearing behind the man. "Not until you answer some questions." Joe realized that Frank had gone out the broken bedroom window and circled around to the front of the cottage.

The man's face lost the angry expression he'd

used on Joe, and he raised his hands in the air. "All right, all right, Officer," he said. "I'll tell you what you want to know."

"Good, go inside," Frank said.

The man walked into the cottage and sat down in a spindly wooden chair with a broken arm. Frank walked in the front door, and Joe joined him in front of the man.

"Wait a minute," the man said. "You're not the police."

"It doesn't matter who we are," Joe said. "You're still going to talk to us."

The man looked from Joe to Frank and back to Joe. He seemed to decide that they had the upper hand, and shrugged his shoulders as he leaned back against the table. To guarantee there'd be no surprises, the Hardys tied the man's wrists and his ankles with rope. Then Frank sat down and asked the most obvious question. "Are you Baron Brighthall?"

"I suppose I am in a way," the man said, "but probably not the one you mean. I am John Brighthall, Baron Jackson Brighthall's brother. Jackson has been dead for many years and was the rightful heir to this estate."

"And you've been creeping around as his ghost all this time?" Joe said. "Why?"

"I have my reasons, and they're none of your concern," Brighthall said.

"I'm afraid you're wrong there," Frank said.

"And it will be just as much of a concern to Police Officer Chester, too."

"All right, all right, you don't have to threaten me," Brighthall said, waving his hand in the air. "I'm tired of haunting, anyway. I'm tired of this whole search. I've been doing this for more than ten years. Maybe it's time I turned in my bow and arrows for another gig."

"What search?" Frank asked. The man indeed sounded very tired and as if he'd given up.

"For the treasure," Brighthall said. "My brother always talked about a fabulous treasure buried on the estate. When he died, I decided to find it. But I've come to believe it never existed, that it was just a hoax my brother played on me."

"We heard that your brother was murdered," Joe said, "and that the murderer has never been found. Do you know who did it? Did *you* do it?"

"Of course not," Brighthall said. "My brother and I weren't exactly friends, but we *were* family. He was not murdered. It was an accident. We had a fight—a physical fight—over the treasure. I swear it was an accident, but there were no witnesses."

"Why didn't you tell all this to the police?" Joe asked.

"I didn't think they'd believe me," Brighthall said. "So I fled to Newfoundland, where I hid out for years. I would come over occasionally and search for the treasure. A couple of trespassers came across me

once, and they assumed I was my brother's ghost. When I read the story in the local paper, I decided to capitalize on the idea in order to scare people off the estate. When I heard that Alan Horton had paid off the delinquent taxes and was the new owner, I was determined to find the treasure before he did."

"Do you know where Alan is?" Frank asked.

For the first time, Brighthall seemed to be nervous, edgy. "Uh, no—not exactly," he said.

The Hardys closed in, standing very close to the man in the chair. "What do you know?" Frank asked, his fists clenched at his sides.

"There's this guy," Brighthall said. "He caught me on the property. I paid him to keep quiet. But he didn't want only money. When he found out who I was, he made me give him all my maps— maps of the marble mine beneath the property and of the estate itself, including diagrams of the house. He's coming back tonight to get the money. It took me a while to get it together."

Frank reached in his pocket and pulled out the photo of Bruce MacLaren that Joe had printed from his computer. "Is this the guy?"

Brighthall squinted at the photo. "No, my man's clean-shaven—no beard, no mustache."

"Imagine this guy without the red fuzz," Joe said.

"Okay, yeah, that could be him. What's going on? What's he done?"

"He may have kidnapped Alan Horton," Frank

said. "And since you gave him the maps he might have used to pull off the crime, that makes you an accessory. You can go to prison for a long time as an accessory to kidnapping—or worse."

"And when they figure in that you might have killed your brother, too . . ." Joe added.

"Okay, what do you want me to do?" Brighthall asked. "I don't know what happened to Alan—although I hope it's nothing bad. He's really a pretty decent fellow. Puts on a whale of a show."

"When is MacLaren coming by?" Frank asked.

"Eight thirty."

"That's an hour and a half from now. We've got time to set a trap for him. But first we have to make sure we find out where Alan is. You've got to help us and, by doing so, you'll help yourself, too."

Frank called Officer Chester and told him about Brighthall. He also laid out his idea for capturing MacLaren and finding Alan. "He wants to talk to you," Frank said, holding his cell phone next to Brighthall's ear.

"Yes, yes," Brighthall said, nodding his head. "Yes, I swear I will. I'm offended that my maps were used to hurt the Hortons. I just wanted to scare them away. I never meant for any harm to come to them. Yes, I will."

Frank took the phone back, spoke to the policeman for another few minutes, and then hung up. "We're going to untie you now," he said, loosening

the knot on one of Brighthall's ropes. "Officer Chester said you two have a deal. He's on his way out, and should be here in about forty-five minutes."

"Don't worry, I'm not going to run," Brighthall said, standing and flexing his arms. "I'm in this to the finish. What do I do first?"

"Just practice your act," Frank said. "Remember—you tell MacLaren that you found Joe in the cottage and he's figured out everything. Tell him that you know he's kidnapped Alan, and suggest that the two of you kidnap Joe, too. Tell him that Joe's pretty well-known in America and might be worth a healthy ransom. You have to convince him to kidnap Joe and take him to the same place he's keeping Alan. We'll do the rest."

Brighthall began pacing the room, rehearsing his lines and adding appropriate facial expressions and gestures.

"You're sure you're okay with this?" Frank asked his brother.

"Absolutely," Joe said. "We've got to find Alan and get him home alive and safe. You'll have to do the bandage." He dropped his jeans and leaned over the table. He heard Frank ask if he was ready. Joe gritted his teeth and nodded.

With one quick yank, Frank peeled back a corner of the large taped dressing on Joe's calf. Then he reached in his sports bag and took out his GPS. He placed the tracker on Joe's calf, making sure it was

far from his healing wound. Then he rolled the tape down and closed the dressing, concealing the tracker.

His teeth still tightly clenched, Joe pulled up his jeans and nodded to Frank. Then Frank tied Joe's wrists with a slipknot so that he could get out of the binding quickly if he had to.

"Remember," Frank said to Joe and Brighthall, "just yell if you get in trouble. The police will have people stationed all along the road back to the house; a roadblock at the main gate; and a couple of boats in the lake. They'll be covering you all the way."

"Do we know where the Hortons are?" Joe asked.

"They're at the stadium," Frank said. "Officer Chester said that when it didn't rain after all, they decided to go on with the games."

"I'm going out now," Frank said. "I'll catch Officer Chester and he can wait in the woods with me. It's really dark out, so it'll be perfect."

"Don't forget the shortcut back to the house that I told you about," Brighthall said.

"I won't," Frank answered. "And don't you forget your lines—and whose side you're on now." He turned to his brother, tied with the fake binding. "See you soon," he said.

"Soon," Joe repeated.

At 8:15 Frank hid in the birch woods and waited. *Where* is *he?* Frank wondered as the minutes passed. *Officer Chester should have been*

here by now. Finally, he heard footsteps coming down the trail. *It's about time,* he thought. *MacLaren will be here any minute.*

Frank stretched up to get a better viewpoint, but even in the dark he could tell it was not Officer Chester coming toward the cottage.

Stomping down the trail was Bruce MacLaren.

15 The Gallant Knights

Frank ducked back into the protective cover of the woods. *He's early,* he thought. *MacLaren's early.* Frank could see the cottage, but he couldn't hear what was being said. Only ten minutes passed before the door opened again. Joe walked up the trail, followed by the clean-shaven Bruce MacLaren.

Frank waited until they were out of sight. Then he raced into the cottage.

"He bought it all," Brighthall told him. "Said he was going up to the house and he'd be back in touch tomorrow."

"I can't wait for Officer Chester," Frank said. "I have to move now. Wait for him and bring him up to the house when he gets here. I'm sure MacLaren's going to the secret study, and from there maybe

down to the mine. I'll wait as long as I can before I go after them. You know that house as well as anyone. You'll be able to find us."

Frank checked his GPS receiver and raced to the truck. He used the shortcut and arrived at the house a few minutes before MacLaren and Joe. He waited for Brighthall and Officer Chester as long as he could, but finally had to go inside.

He ducked into Joe's downstairs bedroom and heard two sets of footsteps walk through the kitchen, into the hall, and up the curved staircase. The GPS confirmed that one set belonged to Joe.

Frank followed at a safe distance. He had already guessed where they were going, even without the GPS to tip him off. He waited twenty minutes, then sidled down the upstairs hall and through the hidden door in the back of the closet. Then he stopped at the bottom of the short stairway up to Alan's secret study, straining to hear what was happening in the little room above.

He heard footsteps, then a thud. *That's MacLaren jumping up on the drafting table to pull the switch that opens the pocket door,* Frank guessed.

Creaking, and then more footsteps—this time, faster. *They're heading for the elevator,* he thought. He raced up the steps two at a time, and raced across the small study. Frank stayed out of sight next to the open pocket door until he heard the elevator door close and start to move. Then he raced

down the wide hall, took a deep breath, and carefully stepped onto the top of the elevator as it slid down the chute.

They'll never feel that bounce, he assured himself, remembering the lurching, bumpy ride he and Joe had taken earlier. He held tightly to the cable and rode the roof all the way to the bottom.

The elevator stopped with a shuddering thunk. *Please don't cave in,* Frank thought as marble grit and chunky shards rained down on his head. The door below him opened, and a flashlight beam shot out. There was almost a yard between the elevator and the marble wall. He ducked over to the other side of the roof, in case MacLaren was tempted to look up. When he heard the two sets of footsteps leave the elevator, he relaxed for a minute.

He checked his GPS. Joe had walked straight for several yards, then turned left. Frank slid off the top of the elevator and pulled his penlight from his pocket. Following the light beam and his GPS, he tracked Joe through several tunnels until he heard voices ahead. He stopped and leaned close to the dirty wall so he could hear what they said.

In the room just ahead of Frank, Joe felt the cold marble through his shirt as he leaned against the wall. Alan Horton sat next to him on the floor. They were both tied with their wrists behind their backs, but only Joe knew that his binding was fake.

"This is like a real room," Joe said. There was a makeshift table made from stacked wooden pilings in the center of the round space. An old kerosene lantern sat on top of the stack, and it had actually fired up when MacLaren lit it.

"I hear you're quite an archer," Joe said to MacLaren. "An Olympian, even. Where did you get the fire for the arrow you shot on Friday night?"

"No problem, really," MacLaren answered. "My arrow was already dipped in fuel, so a lighter was all I needed."

"And you're also the one who set me up for the falcon attack in the stables?" Joe asked.

"Of course," MacLaren said with a smarmy smile. "You were the logical choice since you had been such a stunning volunteer in the opening ceremonies. My family has always had falcons, so I know how to handle them. It was easy enough for me to steal one from a local hunter."

"He stole the gauntlet from the trunk in my study," Alan told Joe. "I caught him up there the night before. Remember? Frank was sneaking around that night and said he saw someone at the top of the stairs. Then, when I wanted to show you the gauntlet, it wasn't there. I knew that it had been stolen—and I was sure it was MacLaren."

"Is he the one who called while I was there?" Joe asked.

"No, that was a business call," Alan said.

146

"Don't be modest, Alan," MacLaren said. "This young man deserves to know how you make your living, how you solve puzzles for other people."

"I already know all about it," Joe said. "Is that why you kidnapped him?"

"Of course," MacLaren said. "Alan should fetch me quite a lot of money—either from the people he works *for* . . . or from the people he works *against*. I'll just auction him off to the highest bidder."

"How did you find out about the house, and the hidden study, and the elevator into the mine?" Alan asked MacLaren.

"I have my sources."

"We know all about *him*, too," Joe said. He explained to Alan about the baron's brother and how he was now working with the police. He could tell he had struck a nerve by the way MacLaren's eyes narrowed and glared at him.

"I think you're going to be too much baggage," MacLaren said to Joe. "I have a feeling there's no way the ransom you'd bring me will be worth the problems you'll cause me." He walked over to Joe. "Let's just take a little walk. I'm sure we can find a room for you and you alone down here—one that no one else will ever find. Stand up."

Joe wriggled up to his feet—not an easy task with his hands behind his back and the sharp pains jabbing through his calf. He wiggled his right hand free and waited until MacLaren was just close

enough. Then he brought his fist around from behind his back and delivered a sledgehammer blow up into MacLaren's chin.

"Nice shot," Frank declared as he ran into the room.

MacLaren stumbled back a few feet, then seemed to regain his balance. He hurled his huge body into Frank with a vicious head-butt into his gut. Frank slammed against the marble with a groan. Joe reached into the stack of wood and yanked out a plank. With one well-aimed blow to MacLaren's kidneys, he dropped the man to his knees. Frank delivered a two-fisted wallop to the side of MacLaren's head, and the man toppled onto the floor like a felled tree.

When John Brighthall finally brought Officer Chester and his deputy into the room, MacLaren had regained consciousness, but was tied up with both Alan's and Joe's ropes. There was no need for handcuffs.

The two police officers, Brighthall, and MacLaren took the first elevator ride up. Then they sent the little car back down for the Hardys and Alan.

By the time Frank, Joe, and Alan arrived downstairs in the Horton house, Brighthall and MacLaren were on their way to the police station, and Officer Chester and Shorty had brought Penny and the twins back to the house.

Alan poured goblets of mulled cider for everyone.

"Here's a toast to Frank Hardy and Joe Hardy," he announced, "and I hereby proclaim them Gallant Knights of EagleSpy."

The Hardys gently bowed their heads and smiled. Then they caught the others up to speed.

"That reminds me, Joe," Officer Chester said. "I asked Brighthall how he got into the maze last night. He says he didn't—he was in Newfoundland rounding up money to give to MacLaren."

Reluctantly, Joe told the others about his three A.M. trip through the maze.

"But if Brighthall was in Newfoundland, who did you see in the maze?" Ray asked Joe.

"Wait a minute," Frank said. "Are you saying Joe really did see a *ghost*?"

"Well, it wouldn't be the first time I got a report of a ghost on Cape Breton, that's for sure," Officer Chester said.

"You and Frank have set the baron free, Joe," Kay said matter-of-factly. "Now that you've unmasked his brother, the baron won't have to wander around, haunting the estate. He finally is free—he has a way *out*."

"Well, before he leaves completely," Ray said, turning to Joe, "maybe you can ask your new friend where the buried treasure is!"

"I'll see what I can do," Joe said, winking at his brother.